WALT DISNEY
PICTURES PRESENTS

# HOME
## On The
# RANGE

## The Adventures of a
# Bovine Goddess

By Maggie the Cow with Monique Peterson

**A Welcome Book**

Exceptional thanks to the *Home on the Range* posse
whose contributions made this book possible:
Dale Baer, Michael Baum, Chris Buck,
Susan Butterworth, Pam Coats, Chen Yi Chang,
Leo Chu, Sandro Cleuzo, David Cutler, Alice Dewey,
Will Finn, Maggie Gisel, Joe Grant, Mark Henn,
Suzanne Holmes, Michael Humphries, Karen A. Keller,
Shawn Keller, Mark Kennedy, Michael LaBash,
Sam Levine, James Lopez, Cristy Maltese,
Duncan Marjoribanks, Alan Menken, Chris Montan,
Joe Moshier, Carol Police, Jean-Christophe Poulain,
John Sanford, Glenn Slater, Ann Sorensen,
Mike Surrey,  Mark Walton, and Marlon West.

—M.P.

The book's producers would also like to thank the
following for their assistance: John Alexander, Kent
Gordon, Doeri Welch Greiner, and Mark Henley at
Feature Animation; Vivian Procopio and Tamara Khalaf
at the Animation Research Library; Tim Lewis and
Natalie Farrey of Disney Publishing Digital Content
Services; Kevin Breen and Barbara Quinn of Walt
Disney Business Affairs & Legal; and Kathleen
Counihan of Medicine Man Gallery, Inc.

Special thanks to Kelley Derr.

**Home on the Range
The Adventures of a Bovine Goddess**

For information, address
Disney Editions
114 Fifth Avenue
New York, New York 10011–5690
www.disneyeditions.com
*Editorial Director:* WENDY LEFKON
*Editor:* JODY REVENSON

Produced by
Welcome Enterprises, Inc.
6 West 18th Street
New York, New York 10011
www.welcomebooks.biz
*Project Manager:* H. CLARK WAKABAYASHI
*Designer:* GREGORY WAKABAYASHI

Library of Congress
  Cataloging-in-Publication Data on file
ISBN 0-7868-5408-1

First Edition
10 9 8 7 6 5 4 3 2 1

Printed in Canada

# Introduction

**Whoa, Nellie!** Before you start thinking this book is just a lot of pretty pictures, let me set you straight on what this book is really about . . . *me!* Well, me and the cast and crew of what would turn out to be a filmmaking experience packed with action and excitement and more than a few surprises. I may have been the one asked to tell the story, but I had more than a little help from my friends and colleagues. You'll find out more about them later.

Let me start by telling you a little about myself. My launch into celebrity started about fifteen years ago, when I surprised everyone in the barnyard by wrangling the crown for Miss Bell Ringer. Overnight, I went from being a dark cow candidate to having a signed film contract, an agent, and a career that I could milk for all it was worth. I became the original Miss Happy Heifer for being the first American bovine beauty to make it on the silver screen, and I've since won the Golden Udder Award three times. It may have been a small step for a cow, but it was a giant step for female kine.

Believe it or not, I've always been more than just a dairy cow, I've been a *diary* cow. I've been keeping journals and scrapbooks of my adventures since I was knee-high to a butter churn. So, you can imagine my excitement when my agent (who knew this about me) called and said that my deal had just become sweeter than cream. He said, "Maggie, you know there's gonna be a book about the making of this film, but there's never been one written through eyes like yours." Honestly, I couldn't have said it better myself. Not only a starring role but also a book for Disney! (And the extra scratch ain't bad, either!)

I brought my laptop with me everywhere. (I have a state-of-the-art hoof-anomic Farmer-in-the-Dell computer.) I kept a journal, took pictures, kept call sheets and other film ephemera, and documented what I could with the help of the cast and crew. Then I handed everything over to a book designer and—voilá!—the adventures of a bovine goddess published for posterity. My costar Grace put it best—it's a behind-the-cow kind of book.

Watching these filmmakers do their magic was the biggest and best roller coaster ride I've ever been on. My eyes nearly popped out of my skull when I saw how the art department transformed a dumpy, deserted town in the middle of nowhere to hustling, bustling Chugwater. And my days in the high desert? I sort of thought I'd be sipping tropical drinks with the producer by the swimming pool. Instead, I was being carted away by rabid, cow-eating prairie dogs! (But, legally I'm not allowed to tell that story.) What I saw with my own eyes is the kind of stuff ballads are made from. And, believe me, we had a lot to sing about around the campfire. One thing's for sure—*Home on the Range* ain't your mother's Western.

**— Maggie the Cow,** April 2004

# Home on the Range

Music by Alan Menken, Lyrics by Glenn Slater

*Out in the land where the men are tough as cactus,*
*Out in the land where the Wild, Wild West was won,*
*Out in the land of the desperado,*
*If yer as soft as an avocado,*
*Yee-ha! Yer guacamole, son!*

*Home, Home,*
*This ain't it pal!*
*Home, Home,*
*Home on the Range.*
*Home, Home,*
*Better go git, pal!*
*You ain't home on the Range.*

*Out in the land where the weak are*
   *target practice,*
*Home, Home,*
*Home on the Range.*
*Out in the land where they shoot the*
   *mild and meek.*
*Home, Home,*
*Home on the Range.*
*Out where the bad are a whole lot badder,*
*If yer the type with a nervous bladder,*
*Yip! Yow! Yer saddle's gonna reek!*
*'Cause you ain't home on the range,*
*Cowboy—*
*Yer really up a creek!*

Home, Home,
Home on the Range.
Home, Home,
Home on the Range.
Home, Home,
Home on the Range.
Home, Home,
Home on the Range.

# CHAPTER 1
# A Real Cattle Call

These early preproduction drawings gave us all a sense of the story line and the filmmakers' vision.

# Day 1

**My agent called me this afternoon** while I was cruising down the Ventura Freeway. Maggie, he tells me, Disney's looking for a bell ringer for a new picture they're putting together. They need someone cunning and clever. Someone with a wink in her eye and a curl in her lip. Someone sassy and brassy, and udderly gorgeous. Like me!

So after chewing the fat with him, I showed up on the Walt Disney Feature Animation lot to meet the directors, Will Finn and John Sanford. Nice guys. John worked with the Hunchback of Notre Dame and Mulan, and Will worked with Cogsworth on *Beauty and the Beast* and Iago on *Aladdin*, so I know they're used to dealing with, shall we say, *unique* personalities.

They took a look at me, and I took a look at them. Then they said, "We need a leader, the kind who can charge the atmosphere with her mere presence."

So I stood up on my tippy-hooves and belched out, "I'm your bovine, boys."

The contracts were at the lawyer's office the next morning.

# Day 2 I met my costar bovine "angels" today—Mrs. Caloway and Grace. Caloway

seems a bit stiff and proper. Maybe it's the hat she wears. Maybe it's too tight. She's quite the consummate professional, though, and I do look forward to working with her. After all, she's renowned for her roles in *The Milkmaid of Venice*, *Much A-Moo About Nothing*, and *Madame Bovinary*. Not surprising, she's trained by one of the best: Duncan Marjoribanks, whose protégés include Sebastian from *The Little Mermaid*, Abu from *Aladdin*, and Ratcliffe from *Pocahontas*.

Grace is about as 180 as you can get from Caloway. While Caloway is solid and steady as she goes (like a rectangular-shaped ship), Grace is delicate. The way she's built—it's like her little feet barely touch the ground. Which makes sense because she's a real dreamer. Definitely innocent and maybe a little naive—like she's never been off the farm. No wonder Caloway and I immediately felt protective of her. But, like Caloway, she's also a true professional, and it's paid off—Best Supporting Actress in *Chi-cow-go*. Plus, she starred in the box-office hits *American Cowpie* and *Bridget Jones's Dairy*.

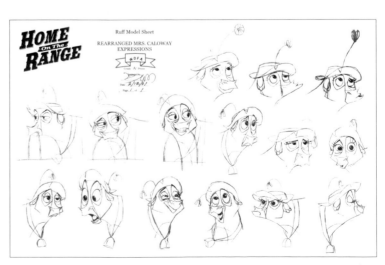

Her acting coach is Mark Henn. He worked with Ariel in her *Little Mermaid* role (big stretch there with the tail and all), as well as Jasmine, Belle, and Mulan (my Friday-night mud bath pals) and Young Simba before he was *The Lion King*.

Speaking of coaches, I'm happy to give credit here to my own acting coach, Chris Buck. Not only did he develop my acting chops (which he also helped do for Pocahontas and Tarzan), but he also gave me some great physical exercises that helped me stay limber and agile. I'm a big-boned cow, no doubt about that. But his workout advice gave me an athletic, hefty grace on screen which would serve me well in this film. In short, Chris really knew how to draw the best out of me.

After lunch, I grazed around with the casting director, Mary Hidalgo, while she, the directors Will Finn and John Sanford, and Alice Dewey, the producer, sat through more auditions. Alice worked on *Aladdin*, *The Lion King*, and *Hercules*, so I wasn't surprised to see a lot of blue-ribbon potential in the corral.

Some were real whinny-ers, but most were real winners.

**BUUURP! Ahhh! That was goooood! Unfortunately, I don't think Caloway was too fond of my bovine belching skills. And she calls herself a cow....**

These little guys gave me a run for my money at the salad bar every day. They also kept grumpy ol' Jeb in character by jumping him every once in a while.

The filmmakers knew this was Pearl the moment they laid eyes on her. Strong and loving—she made us all feel like kin.

You'd never know it just by looking at him but this sweet little goat was transformed when he assumed the role of Jeb. A curmudgeon par excellence.

One tough bunch! Nobody messed with these chicks.

No offense to Rusty . . .
but I'm really more of a cat cow.

The guy who played Abner got the job because the directors loved the mustache. The color was wrong, but that's nothing a little hair dye couldn't take care of.

The chickens were a nice bunch but looked like they had never been to an audition before. Then one of them opened her mouth and the role of Audrey was born.

There was a duck who danced his way through the audition. He was so bad, he got the job.

This old guy read the part of the Sheriff like he was born to play it. In fact, he was so convincing when he said he was sorry for delivering Pearl the bad news that we all felt like we had to cheer him up.

One who started as a whinny-er but ended up a winner was a horse named Buck. It seems his agent had told him that the horse would get top billing in this film, so he was caught a little off guard when he found out that Caloway, Grace, and I were to be the bovine bosses of *Home on the Range*. He was arrogant and cocky and, in truth, not very likable. He really needed to cool his saddle a bit.

Buck's acting coach, Mike Surrey, took him aside for a little chat. Like the other coaches involved, Surrey had a great resumé. He'd started by working with Lumiere on *Beauty and the Beast*, and with Aladdin. Later he worked with Timon on *The Lion King*, Clopin on *The Hunchback of Notre Dame*, and Terk on *Tarzan*. Once he got Buck to calm down a little, Surrey told him to use his natural cockiness but to be a more sympathetic character. The story crew had written a terrific part for Buck—a horse who feels he's stuck in a nine-to-five job but who wants more adventure. He's a dreamer who wants a greater destiny for himself. Surrey wanted Buck to have a good time with it.

That little talk worked because Buck nailed the audition and sent the other horses being considered for the part out to pasture. He turned out to be a lot of fun to work with but still full of himself, to be sure. I kept my eye on him all throughout the shoot.

These horses (left and above right) were among those considered for the role, but Buck won out in the end.

# Day 4

**When it comes to Westerns**—even an upside-down comedy like this one—a good villain is hard to find. And, boy, was Slim a hard one to nail to the fence post. I'll say this much: it wasn't pretty. There was one with real promise who had starred in *My Big Fat Creek Wedding* and *XXXL Saddles*, but the filmmakers were a little concerned he might have a bit too much, uh, screen presence, if you get what I mean! Besides which, I had it in my contract that *I* would be the biggest star in this film. It took a full day of auditions until well after sundown but they eventually got their man—who did a burning lasso trick in his audition that clinched the deal. (We're still trying to figure that one out.) His singing voice really impressed everyone. He had recently done a stint on Broadway as the lead in *Even Villains Sing the Blues*. Besides which, his work in the theater made him adept at the quick wardrobe changes which would be integral to his role in *Home on the Range*.

But the guys they cast as Slim's henchmen really gave me the willies. They were the meanest, ugliest bunch of rustlers I've ever laid my big brown eyes on. I don't know where they found these guys. I think they just put up open audition posters from one Western town to another, and these are the guys who answered the call.

Then the *real* Willie Brothers Gang showed up with their horses. It's pretty amazing how they succeed in being able to pull the wool over everyone's eyes—especially their own. I watched one of the brothers go into the wardrobe trailer and come out with a new getup. The other brothers had no idea they were looking at the third of their trio. Wish I could do that with a few of the heifers in my herd.

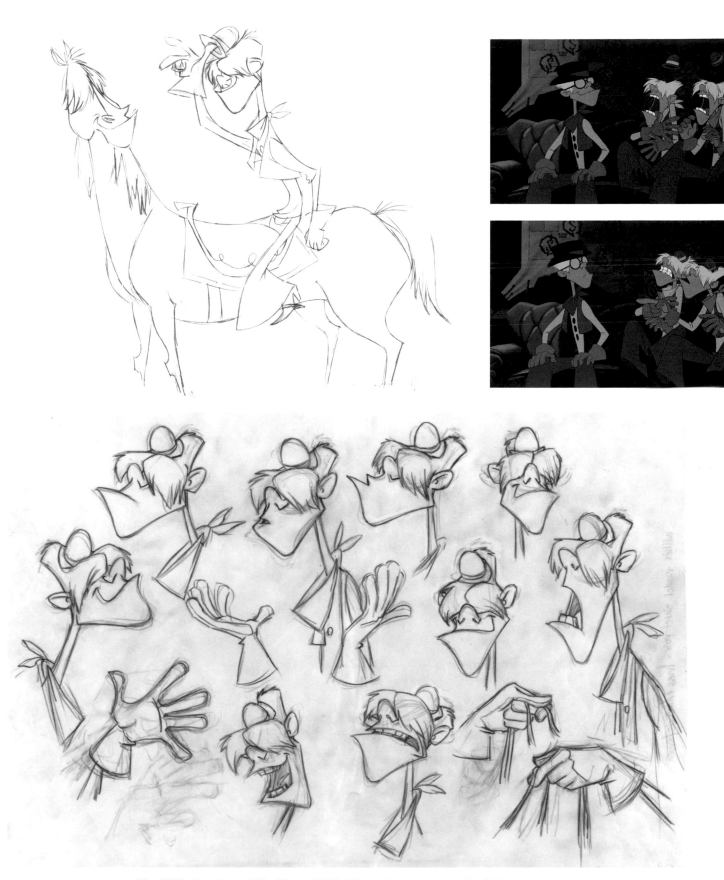

The Willie Brothers: Bill, Gil, and Phil. The only way you could tell them apart
was by the color of their bandannas and hatbands.

# Day 5

**It's the end of the week,** the directors have rounded up their cast. From the looks of all the head shots, I knew we'd be in for a rollicking, rough-and-tumble showdown.

# Cast of Characters

**Maggie**

**Mrs. Caloway**

**Grace**

**Buck**

**Alameda Slim**

**Willie Brothers**

**Rico**

**Pearl**

**Abner**

**Sheriff**

**Rusty**

24

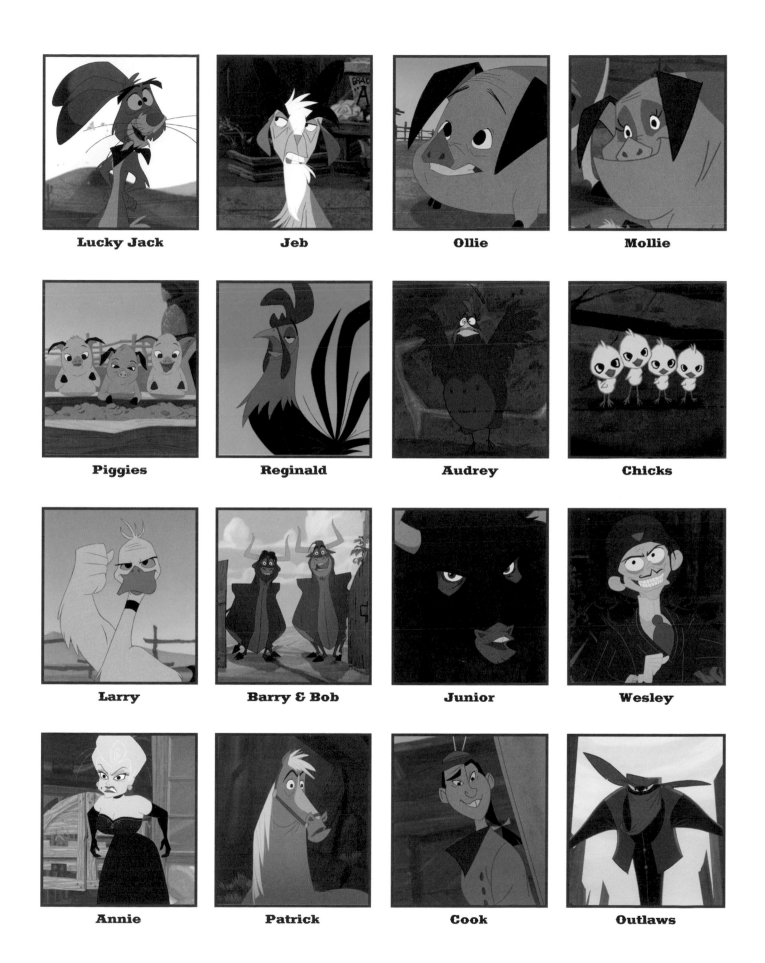

Lucky Jack

Jeb

Ollie

Mollie

Piggies

Reginald

Audrey

Chicks

Larry

Barry & Bob

Junior

Wesley

Annie

Patrick

Cook

Outlaws

25

# CHAPTER 2
# Oh, Give Me a Place

# Day 7

**One thing that impressed me right off** the bat with this team of filmmakers was their desire to immerse themselves into the Old West. These folks were living, breathing, reading, watching, singing, and eating anything evocative of the era: clothing, homes, vehicles, dust. Everything from grass to grits. (Mmm!) The filmmakers even set up a lending library for everyone in the cast and crew. Now, *that's* entertainment!

## Library Selections

### Best Westerns
*The Searchers*
*Shane*
*Silverado*
*High Noon*
*Unforgiven*
*The Man Who Shot Liberty Valance*
*Red River*
*The Culpepper Cattle Company*
*Monte Walsh*
*Lonely Are the Brave*
*Rio Bravo*
*The Cowboys*
*Big Country*

### Disney Picks
*Sleeping Beauty*
*101 Dalmatians*
*Alice in Wonderland*
*Peter Pan*
*Cinderella*
*Toot, Whistle, Plunk, Boom*
*The Sword in the Stone*
*Pigs Is Pigs*
*Pecos Bill*
*Every Boy Has a Horse*
*Johnny Appleseed*

### Cowboy Literature
*Lonesome Dove* by Larry McMurtry
*The Virginian* by Owen Wister
*Little Big Man* by Thomas Berger
*The Outlaw Josey Wales* by Forrest Carter
*Gone to Texas* by Forrest Carter
*The Trail to Seven Pines* by Louis L'Amour
*Riders of the Purple Sage* by Zane Grey

Our crew rides in high country (above)
on a cattle round-up the day before the drive.

Chuck wagon brings our grub (top right).
Make way!

# Day 8 They told me this movie was going to be "all about the cows," and they

weren't kidding. But when I showed up for a preliminary script reading, I noticed a few
people were a little skittish around me, and it became pretty obvious pretty quick that what
this film team needed was some serious up close and personal time with cows. A whole
herd of them. So, of course, being an expert on the subject of all things bovine, I took
matters into my own hooves and talked to the team.

"You need locations—I know cow country. Leave it to me, I'll show you the best vistas in
the West. Not to mention the best dairy farms and county fairs this side of the Mississippi."

They said go for it, so I passed them the name and number of my travel agent, Steers &
Stripes Westward Travel.

Art Director David Cutler pauses as he pushes strays into the herd.

Break time!

# Day 20 They wanted cows—they got 'em. Thanks to my connections, the whole crew just came back from an autumn old time cattle drive. Too bad Grace and Caloway missed out—I found out that Grace always spends the week before a film shoot at a yoga retreat, and Caloway's taping the last episode of a new miniseries for the BBC (Bovine Broadcasting Channel).

We spent a week in gorgeous Wyoming, seeing the countryside from 12,000 feet, which is the cattle's summer home, all the way down to the winter retreat at 4,000 feet. We were in the heart of cowboy country, and these city slickers were in for a long ride. I think our lyricist, Glenn Slater, spent more time outdoors in seven days than he has in the last seven months in New York City. But these high-powered multitaskers bit the bullet as we all left our laptops and cell phones behind to capture the true, timeless cowboy experience. And when you're riding on horseback (or kicking up your hooves, in my case) for more than eight hours a day, there's not a whole lot else to do. So, I listened to the story crew toss ideas back and forth while the visual development artists soaked up all the scenery, color, and textures for the look of the film. And, we were never without music. Other than chow time, the best times were sitting around the campfire at night, singing along with some wonderful cowboy balladeers.

The crew poses on horseback before heading the herd down the mountain.

**Composer Alan Menken (below left) shows his horsemanship.**

**Producer Alice Dewey (below right) keeps things moving forward.**

From: Alice Dewey
To: Maggie the Cow <bovinegoddess@moo.cow>
Date: Tuesday, October 23, 2001 8:37 AM
Subject: Cattle Drive

Wed, Oct 24, 2001   10:01 AM

This was a wonderful experience. Going on this cattle drive really helped us to learn a thing or two about life out on the plains in those days. Eating dried foods off tin plates and drinking from tin cups gave us a bit of the real feel of the time, since our film is set in the 1880s. I loved seeing the landscape from above the timberline, through the pine trees, through the chaparral, all the way down to the high desert. It gave us a great sense of the West. And the colors—so incredibly rich!

Everyone slept so peacefully under the stars. But when the ranch foreman woke us up at sunrise with a gunshot instead of an alarm clock, you never saw twelve people in their sleeping bags scurry into their pants so fast! But the view was breathtaking: the sun was a red line along the mountains—dark crimson red—and the rest of the sky was so black.

Throughout the week there were no cars or telephone poles. I don't even think we saw a single airplane. I really felt as if we had gone back in time.

Great idea, Maggie!
Alice

# Day 22 **As soon as we got back from the cattle drive,** we knew from the

get-go that there would be plenty of building sets and backdrops. It turns out that we'd be

filming on at least half a dozen locations—all of which were gonna need a little sprucing up (to say the least). The art director and the artists and painters took in the lay of the land. Sure, this movie is all about the cows (obviously), but it's gotta have style. And when it comes to art direction, David

Cutler is the man. He previously worked on *The Rescuers Down Under* and *The Little Mermaid*. For this film, David developed a style that's graphic and cartoony with a very saturated palette—a real gritty version of the West. One with a retro, hard-edged feel. Something more like me—angular with a selective use of curves.

# Day 24

**I tagged along with the art department today,** checking out galleries and exhibits featuring contemporary and vintage Western artists. We looked at work by Maynard Dixon, Ed Mell, Victor Higgins, Samuel Coleman, and the Hudson River School, as well as paintings by Louis Akin, Thomas Moran, and Albert Tissandier. We also pored over the work of earlier Disney artists such as Mary Blair and Eyvind Earle. On top of that, we looked at the work of 20th-century masters Henri Matisse and Vincent van Gogh. Boy, were my hooves tired!!

I asked Carol Police, the film's Layout Stylist, how looking at old paintings was going to help her build a set. She summed it up for me in one word: mayonnaise.

Now, here's a woman who speaks my language! I love a person who can think with her gut. So, we chewed the cud as she spelled out her recipe.

She explained that the ingredients could be divided into several basic categories: scale, shape, light, and texture. Then you take the best of elements of the artists whose work was studied and create a fresh new feeling for *Home on the Range*.

On these pages we've juxtaposed works from some of the artists who inspired the *Home on the Range* crew with examples of their own visual development art.

## Scale

- Emphasize the sense of scale. See works of Dixon (left), Mell, and Coleman.
- Silhouette objects in the foreground to evoke an atmospheric perspective.
- Use verticality of the Western landscape to pit large against small.
- Focus on a very low horizon to push the presence of the sky and the clouds. Focus on a high horizon to emphasize the depth of a canyon.

34

## Shape
– Use interesting shapes to draw you into the landscape. A repeated use of the same shape, patterns of shapes, or a variety of size shows playfulness. See works of Henri Matisse or Mary Blair (above).

## Light
– Incorporate bold shadows for staging and composition of landscapes, like Dixon.
– Use clear, simple lighting to emphasize graphic boldness over realistic light, like Mell (below).

## Texture
– Incorporate large, simple areas of texture and overlaying textures to evoke a feeling of richness and complexity, not superficiality.
– Create a sense of space and richness, like Vincent van Gogh or Eyvind Earle (above).

# Day 27 After spending days grazing through

some of the best countryside the West has to offer and
watching the sets come together, I couldn't believe my big
brown eyes when we came across a dry, dusty dump of a
town. Then I found out this was going to be Chugwater.
Looks more like Drought City to me. And by the looks of
the outlaws who ride around these parts, I don't think it's
the kind of place for a nice Jersey girl like me.

Among the locations we visited was the
deserted town of Calico. It served as an
inspiration for the design of Chugwater.

I found out that Carol Police isn't the only artist who
thinks of art in gustatorial terms. When I got to the buffet
trough for lunch, I found the art department crew playing with the food!

I quickly learned that background painting department supervisor Cristy Maltese was
behind all of this. She had some explaining to do! I found her by a bucket of shucked corn.
It was all ears, and so was I.

Cristy told me that when the crew first got together, she wanted them to think about creating the backgrounds as if they were a craft project. She asked them to remember when they were in kindergarten and cut out big construction-paper shapes, and glued dried beans and macaroni on them. (Yummy!) This would inspire them in making the backgrounds look dimensional. And they also needed to portray differences in perspective. She explained how you could do this by painting a very angular, two-dimensional shape and laying textures on top of it, which makes it appear three-dimensional. She called this "faceting." Then they scanned these textures into the computer, because maybe half of the backgrounds would be painted digitally. Tamara Boutcher, the production manager, told me another way they achieved a dimensional look was with a computer program called "Make Sticky." Traditional art was projected or "stuck" onto 3-D shapes. This worked best for moving camera shots.

At that point, Cristy pulled out a sketchbook and showed me how her crew created these textures. On the big scenic backdrops, they used watercolor paper and corrugated

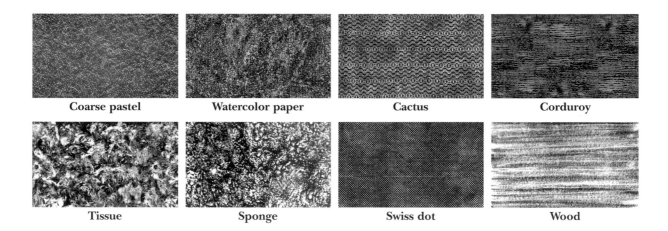

**Coarse pastel**      **Watercolor paper**      **Cactus**      **Corduroy**

**Tissue**      **Sponge**      **Swiss dot**      **Wood**

cardboard to create prints in the same way I'd use a rubber stamp. They did the same thing for the interiors, too, creating textures from a variety of fabrics, lace, sponges, dry brushes, and even tissues.

They painted the paper, fabric, or other material with a different color and laid it on top of the background. Then, when the material is removed, there's a really unique-looking ground plane. They did this a few times, making several layers to create a look that appears authentic.

As they were sprucing up this barren wasteland of a town with some high desert vegetation, I got to see how a little chalk and sponge could do the trick. I took a page from Cristy's sketchbook. Literally!

See here (bottom right) how sponge and watercolor paper were used on the rock surfaces, with drybrush dragged across to create striations.

Part way through the production, the background department made a surprising discovery. The painters could match the same organic look by scanning the textures and using a computer stylus rather than a paintbrush. David Steinberg, the film's Associate Producer, told me later that the whole movie required more than 1,500 lavish backgrounds! Ultimately, seventy percent of the film's backgrounds were painted digitally.

42

43

# Day 29

**Pre-light day.** All the locations have been squared away, and the set is dressed for the first day of shooting. The only thing left to do is light it. As I was checking out the doings, I met up with Michael Humphries, a visual development artist. When I marveled at how theatrical and colorful the lighting was, and congratulated him on how his logistics made it come together, he told me how there was no logic involved!

He was doing the lighting based on the mood of the scene versus naturalistic light. According to him, everything should break the rules a bit. (My life story, babe!) By using a

more theatrical approach to lighting, the scenes could be made more interesting. It would be as if we were on stage, using colored lights rather than natural lights.

Of course, I love being in any kind of light, especially the limelight. So now when I'm on-screen, all the lights will be on me! (Does it get much better than that?)

44

# CHAPTER 3
# Horse Opera

## Home on the Range CALL SHEET

**LOCATION: PATCH OF HEAVEN**

| DATE/TIME | SEQ. | DESCRIPTION | CAST |
|---|---|---|---|
| Mon./6:00 A.M. | 1 | Song: "LITTLE PATCH OF HEAVEN" <br> *Musical intro to the farm.* | Caloway, Grace, Pearl, farm animals |
| Tues./8:00 A.M. | 1.5 | MAGGIE MOVES IN <br> *Abner drops off Maggie at Patch of Heaven.* | Maggie, Caloway, Grace, Pearl, Abner, farm animals |
| Tues./11:00 A.M. | 3.5 | LEAVING THE FARM <br> *The cows set off to town with a plan to save the farm.* | Maggie, Caloway, Grace, Pearl, Abner, farm animals |
| Tues./2:00 P.M. | | SET REDRESS | |
| Wed./8:00 A.M. | 3 | PEARL & SHERIFF <br> *The Sheriff delivers foreclosure notice to Pearl.* | Maggie, Caloway, Grace, Pearl, Sheriff, Buck, farm animals |
| Wed./11:00 A.M. | 14 | BACK ON THE FARM <br> *Everyone at Patch of Heaven prepares for foreclosure sale.* | Pearl, farm animals |
| Wed./2:00 P.M. | | TRANSPORT TO CHUGWATER | |

# Day 30 
**First day of shooting**—but not for me! Now, every film script has a number of stops and starts, and this one was no exception. First, the film was going to begin with a narrator who'd explain who everybody was and what was going on. They thought about using Pearl, the owner of Patch of Heaven, for this, or a codgerly hare named Lucky Jack who'd keep being interrupted by Buck. Then, they thought about opening the whole she-bang with the villain, Slim. The directors even thought of opening with a musical number by a tiny butterfly mariachi band. Finally, they decided to start with the central characters—the cows.

This morning, I got the new script pages with yet another major change. Originally, I was going to be one of a trio of leading ladies on the farm, but the directors came up with the idea to make me the new cow on the block. The ensuing friction that they would script in would make for even better character dynamics. And they're right. This reworking offers great possibilities to get the story going in the right direction. I wonder what Will and John will think of next?

So, now that I'm not in what turns out to be an opening musical number on the farm, I looked around for a cozy place to watch the melodic mayhem from, and saw Alan and Glenn waving to me. You didn't have to tell me twice—what better viewing spot than next to the music team!

Alan Menken (music) and Glenn Slater (lyrics) are so talented. When you think Disney music, of course you immediately think Alan Menken—*The Little Mermaid*, *Beauty and the Beast*, *Aladdin*, *Pocahontas*, *The Hunchback of Notre Dame*, *Hercules*. He has a whole stable of Academy Awards, Golden Globes, and Grammys for his work. And Glenn Slater's no slacker. He wrote the lyrics for his first Off-Broadway production while he was still in high school, and there's been no slowing him down ever since. He's currently adapting several films for the Broadway stage. He's so busy, I wonder when he ever gets time to eat!

We snuggled together while the scene unfolded, listening to k.d. lang on the playback as her crooning style harkened us back to an earlier era of sweetness. Glenn whispered in my ear that k.d. just brings pure sunshine to the song, and I agreed. She has a way of taking all the words and turning them into characters and values—the things that you just want to hold onto for dear life because they make you so happy. She brings such an evocative timelessness to the music.

I know I'm going to like working with Pearl. Her acting coach is Mark Henn, just like Grace's. Pearl's got a great range, and I'm not talking about the farm. She can go from being all quiet and emotional in one scene to being ready to take off someone's head like she does with the Sheriff when her farm is threatened. She's a lot of fun and keeps a nice clean farm but someone should follow her around with a bucket to catch all the "g's" she's dropping. She calls everyone "Darlin'."

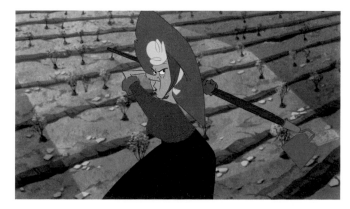

**Pearl came awfully close when she swung that hoe at the Sheriff. She felt just awful about it.**

# Little Patch of Heaven

Music by Alan Menken
Lyrics by Glenn Slater

*I know a place,*
*Pretty as pie,*
*Out where the river bend*
*Hits up with the end o' the sky.*
*It's left of Nebraska,*
*And over a crest,*
*On a little patch of heaven*
*Way out west.*

*Ev'rything's green—*
*Know what I mean?*
*Darlin', it's quite the sweetest sight*
*Thatcha ever done seen.*
*Ain't nothin' much out there—*
*Just life at its best,*
*On that little patch of heaven*
*Way out west.*

*Bees by the dozen*
*Are buzzin'*
*Real peaceful.*
*Ev'ry bluebonnet,*
*Doggone it,*
*Smells nice.*
*Even the tumblin' tumbleweed*
*Slows down to match yer speed*
*On that tiny half-an-acre*
*Of paradise!*

Darlin', I swear—
Once you been there,
There ain't a view
Beneath the blue
That could ever compare!
That only thing missin'
Is you as my guest
On that little patch of heaven
Way out west . . .

Why don'tcha come visit?
There's room in my nest—
On that little patch of heaven
Way out west!

# Day 31 Crisis in the cowshed! While we beauties were getting our

makeup touched up, there were a few problems in the barnyard.
Audrey the chicken was dropping feathers, trying to deliver her
lines. The problem was this: her mouth was too small for her to
belt out all those big lines.

Fortunately, her acting coach James Lopez came to the rescue.
Within no time, he was acting like a Rhode Island Red, and clucking
away with some serious chicken panache. If I
didn't know any better, I would have thought I
was looking at a chicken in a human suit. This man has his
animal moves down pat. After demonstrating a few beak
exercises and some tips on how to ruffle her feathers, Audrey
was like a redrawn character. What pluck!—or should I say,
cluck. She belted out those lines like a true mother hen.

Ollie was the next guinea pig. James got down and dirty in the mud right next to him.
"Ollie," he said, "you've got a great snout, but your mouth gets hidden underneath it and
your words can get muffled. The trick is to tilt your head a little toward the camera and
talk out of the side of your mouth." James taught him
to flap his ear a little when he turned his head. Ollie
got it right away. Such a ham!

But I thought James was most impressive with
the chicks. He got them to show wisdom beyond their
years with nothing more than their eyelids. He stood
before them like a conductor, directing their blinks.
Directors Will and John wanted all the possibilities:
random blinking, one blink, two blinks, no blinks,
and totally synchronized blinks. What peepers!

As the resident curmudgeon, the challenge of Jeb the Goat's character was to make him likeable in spite of his cantankerous personality. His acting coach, Sandro Lucio Cleuzo, had a lot to do with making that work. In fact, I sought out Sandro's advice because, in our first scene together, I'm supposed to squash Jeb! So I wanted us to get off on the right hoof before I turned him into a pancake. Sandro suggested giving him a shiny new can to add to his collection. The idea worked perfectly and the scene went like a dream.

JEB: **They're stew meat.**

OLLIE: **Hurry back!**

Personally, I think Jeb's got a bit of the OCD (his cans have to be arranged *just so*) but most everyone else here thinks of him as that nutty old guy down the block with whom the neighborhood kids are always getting into trouble. But without whom the place just wouldn't be the same.

# Day 32

**The crew needed yesterday afternoon** to redress the farm for Sequence 3 so we filled in the time with a meeting to go over the schedule for our Chugwater scenes. Caloway was practical enough to use one of the cook's pies as a visual aid. But whatever stats that pie chart would have provided, we'll never know. Ollie ate it. (He thought it was a lunch meeting. Lucky swine.) None of us noticed because Jeb and the piggies were arguing over one of his old tin cans. The rest of us were watching Grace try to settle the problem with her usual "organic problem/holistic solution" approach. Since we didn't have time for that I jumped in and handled the situation in my usual diplomatic way.

PIGGIES: **Can hog!**

PIGGIES: **Can hog!  Can hog!**

JEB: **Get off my case, you little cocktail wieners!**

GRACE: **Whoa!**

GRACE: **I'm sensing a lot of negative energy here!**

PIGGIE 1: **That's our can, and Jeb took it!**

PIGGIE 2: **And now he says it's** *his* **can!**

PIGGIES: **Can hog! Can hog!**

JEB: **Possession is 9/10ths of the law!**

JEB: **Doh!**

MAGGIE: **Can it, Jeb!**

MAGGIE: **We'll settle this later!**

You don't even have to know the lines the Sheriff delivers to Pearl about foreclosing the farm to realize this scene is all about bad news. With a new paint job, courtesy of David Cutler's eye for storytelling with color, the place looks more forlorn. A far cry from that happy farm it was before.

As soon as we camera-wrapped out of the farm, we got in our wagon train of trailers and headed out to the newly renovated Chugwater. It was a six-hour cattle drive from Pearl's farm, and we pulled up to the outskirts of town right around dusk. Even though the place has been spruced up by the scenics, it still feels like the kind of place you don't want to be alone in at night.

Maybe it has something to do with the mountains and canyons out yonder, but sound sure travels funny out here. I know it's probably just the wind, but it's eerie all the same. It almost sounds like a haunting yodel.

## Home on the Range CALL SHEET

LOCATION: **CHUGWATER** (REVISED)

| DATE/TIME | SEQ. | DESCRIPTION | CAST |
|---|---|---|---|
| Thur./9:00 A.M. | | SET REHEARSAL | Maggie, Caloway, Grace |
| Thur./10:30 A.M. | 5.5 | BUCK & RUSTY<br>*Buck learns Rico is coming to town.* | Buck, Rusty, Sheriff, Morse |
| Thur./1:00 P.M. | 5.7 | COWS MEET BUCK<br>*Maggie, Caloway, and Grace find out how much they need to save the farm.* | Maggie, Caloway, Grace, Buck, Rusty, Annie, Pappy |
| Thur./3:00 P.M. | 5.6 | COWS IN TOWN<br>*The cows arrive in town.* | Maggie, Caloway, Grace, Buck, townspeople |
| Sat./8:00 A.M. | 5.6 | COWS IN TOWN<br>*Pick up scene in town.* | Maggie, Caloway, Grace, Buck, townspeople |
| Sat./10:00 A.M. | 5.6 | COWS IN TOWN<br>*The cows go to what they think is the Sheriff's office and end up in a saloon fight.* | Maggie, Caloway, Grace, Buck, townspeople, Annie, saloon dancers, patrons |
| Mon./8:00 A.M. | 6 | BOUNTY HUNTING<br>*Rico arrives. The cows decide to collect bounty on Alameda Slim. Rico hires Buck.* | Maggie, Caloway, Grace, Buck, Rusty, Rico, Sheriff, cowboys, cook |

# Day 33 Our first day shooting in Chugwater wasn't what I expected. Now, Will

Finn and John Sanford are the kind of directors you really hope for on a film. They're always thinking, always experimenting with ideas to enrich the characters and the story. We tried a lot of different stuff in rehearsals and still continue to even on the set.

Today, Will and John asked me to try a little something without Caloway's knowledge. The directors came up with the idea of a real confrontation between me and Caloway—down and dirty in the muddy streets of Chugwater. But they weren't sure Caloway would be up for it, given how proper she is and all. Well, we all knew that Caloway has a thing about her hat. She wears her hat the way she wears responsibility—all on her own. Nobody else touches the hat. Will and John didn't even have to explain to me what they wanted me to do.

While Grace and I were clowning around with the pot, pan, and colander props we'd be wearing as hats in a later scene, I suddenly pinched Caloway's precious little flower chapeau pretending that I wanted to try it on. Unfortunately, it slipped from my hoof and *accidentally* fell into the mud. Uh-oh! Caloway charged at me like a raging bull. Any other time, I'd have been impressed to see a display worthy of the streets of Pamplona, but naturally I had to defend myself. I showed her my best cowpuncher moves, and before I knew it, we were mud wrestling. Caloway and I weren't the only ones to get soiled. At one point, someone yelled, "COWFIGHT!" and Rusty came out to have a look-see at just the wrong moment. The directors had the cameras on us the whole time and got it all on film.

Once Caloway had time to calm down, the directors showed us the video playback. Wrestling fans would have been proud. It was spectacular. Even Caloway applauded the idea and its results. Especially since she still gets to wear the hat.

Caloway, Grace, and I had just finished all our street shots in Chugwater for the day when, suddenly, the directors wanted to up the production value by giving us more screen time. What had started out as two separate shots of me and the gals, enjoying the sarsaparilla trough in front of the saloon, then chatting in front of the Sheriff's office,

turned into a roaming conversation between these two buildings through the streets of Chugwater.

So Caloway, Grace, and I worked the *Moo York Times* crossword puzzle while they rewrote the scene.

LAYOUT DEPT. DRAWING

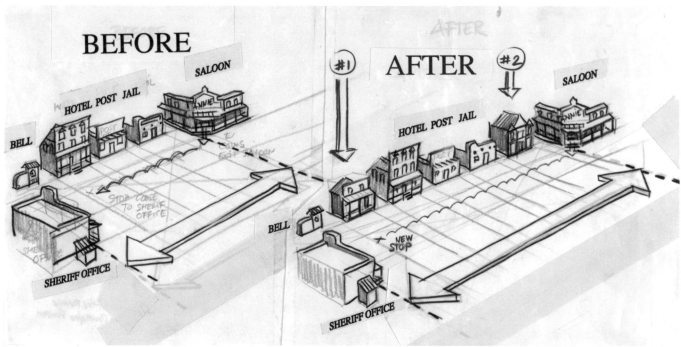

Originally there were just three buildings between the saloon and the sheriff's office.
The Layout Department quickly added two more buildings, one on each end.

By the time the script had been retooled, we came up against another problem: it took us longer to deliver our lines than it took us to walk the distance. What we needed was more than a single building to mosey past—we needed more *town*. It just wasn't going to look good if we kept walking past the same yellow house!

Jean-Christophe Poulain, the head of Layout, helped resolve the situation. The crew designed new houses and combined them with the ones already in place. They also figured out how to turn what was twenty scenes into forty and still save some scenes already in the can.

More unsung heroes whose praises I'm glad to sing.

# Day 34

**The extra time needed** for set building made a long day for us. Chugwater's no Virginia City, but we amused ourselves, nonetheless. While Rusty and Buck had a little mano a mano playing tic-tac-toe, Caloway, Grace, and I decided to have a leisurely visit with the Craft Service crew. The cook sure knows how to pack a good salad bar! I've been working on some of the best chow I've had since I starred in the romance, *Chocolat Lait*. Mmmmm. No doubt that gave me the edge at the spittoon. They sure didn't expect a cowgirl would ever outspit them in distance and marksmanship!

Then Buck came outside after a costume fitting. He had the gumption to show up wearing his own "vintage" mailbag. You should have seen him strutting around in his new duds as if he were on parade in some Annie Oakley stage show. Caloway, Grace, and I were all atwitter when Buck happened upon us. He made some wisecrack about us holding a dairy convention and his taking a pound of butter and a pint of cream. I got him back good, making fun of his precious mailbag: "Well, if it isn't the Phony Express!"

She shoots! She scores!

Buck and I did a lot of verbal sparring during the making of the film. But it was all in fun. To be honest, I did enjoy getting under his hide once in a while.

# Day 35 It was so exciting to be on set today. Chugwater

was teeming with extras. The fight choreographers were duking it out
with the cowboys in Annie's Saloon before we bovine angels got into a
Wild West Smackdown with Annie's burly cancan girls.

I thought it was going to be a real mess to clean up after each
take, but it turned out that wasn't the case. All the breakables,
throwables, and splashables would be handled in Visual Effects.

After we finished the scene, I got the dirty lowdown from
the master behind the magic, Marlon West, who had been watching

our performance. I call him "Newton," because he's always talking about how he deals with gravity.

In this case, he and his team would be dealing with the thrown bottles, the flying chips and peanuts, the sloshing liquid, the props breaking and falling—in *effect* (ha-ha!) any item that isn't on a character or that leaves a character's hands or hooves.

**Day 37** **Some of the coolest stuff** that Marlon and his crew whipped up was all the digital dust. Sure, dust is dust, and in this film, there's a heck of a lot of it. But the visual effects team handled that dust as if it were one of the actors. And in the scene when Rico comes to town, nothing could be truer. The greatest dust story ever told

is when Rico rides into Chugwater and the dust rolls in and billows up, laying the groundwork, so to speak, for the bounty hunter's grand entrance. The dust has such a presence that it just about knocks the Sheriff plum off his chair, and you can't see nothing

but his dusty, blurry silhouette. Of course, his acting coach Sandro Cleuzo choreographed the Sheriff's moves to perfection. Even so, that dust is so mean and nasty, the Sheriff has to keep a firm grip on his hat to keep that dirt cloud from whisking it away altogether.

That's *Rico* dust.

When the dust finally settled, there stood Rico. None of us had seen him at the earlier auditions. Our jaws dropped, and we all laid eyes on the biggest, baddest bounty hunter we'd ever seen. That man is one long drink of water, if I do say so myself.

Well, you would need that much water to keep you from choking on that much dust!

Rico was definitely mysterious. Caloway thought he was a bit creepy. Grace, always the one to think the best of someone, thought Rico was the strong, sensitive type. One

thing we'd heard was that he was Buck's hero. We were kind of curious to see how Buck—Mr. Legend-in-his-own-mind—would act around someone he idolized. Before we knew it, Buck was right there and had launched into his "hey, look at me" routine while Rico and the sheriff were talking. When it came time to do the scene where he gets picked to be Rico's horse, he wept when Rico put his saddle on him. You'd think

he'd just won a beauty contest. Who would have guessed that the ol' buckaroo had a sensitive side? Buck was so happy when the two of them rode off into the sunset together, I felt like I needed to remind him this was a comedy, not a romance.

 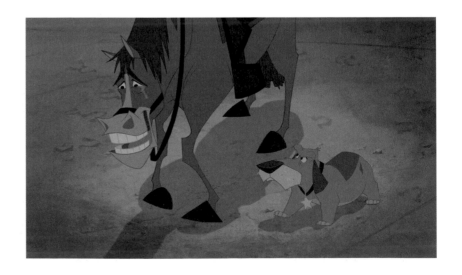

Well, Buck and Rico actually *did* ride off into the open western wilderness. They wanted to get a head start on the next location. Not me. I convinced Caloway and Grace to stick with me and follow the chuck wagon. The crew was busy striking the set, turning Chugwater back into the desolate town that it had been before. Somehow, this town suddenly seemed even lonelier than when I first saw it. So, knowing that we'd be caravanning out of here at the crack of dawn, I decided to call it a day. I retired to my air-conditioned trailer with my 500-channel HDTV and a pint of my favorite Alfalfa 'n' Cream frozen yogurt.

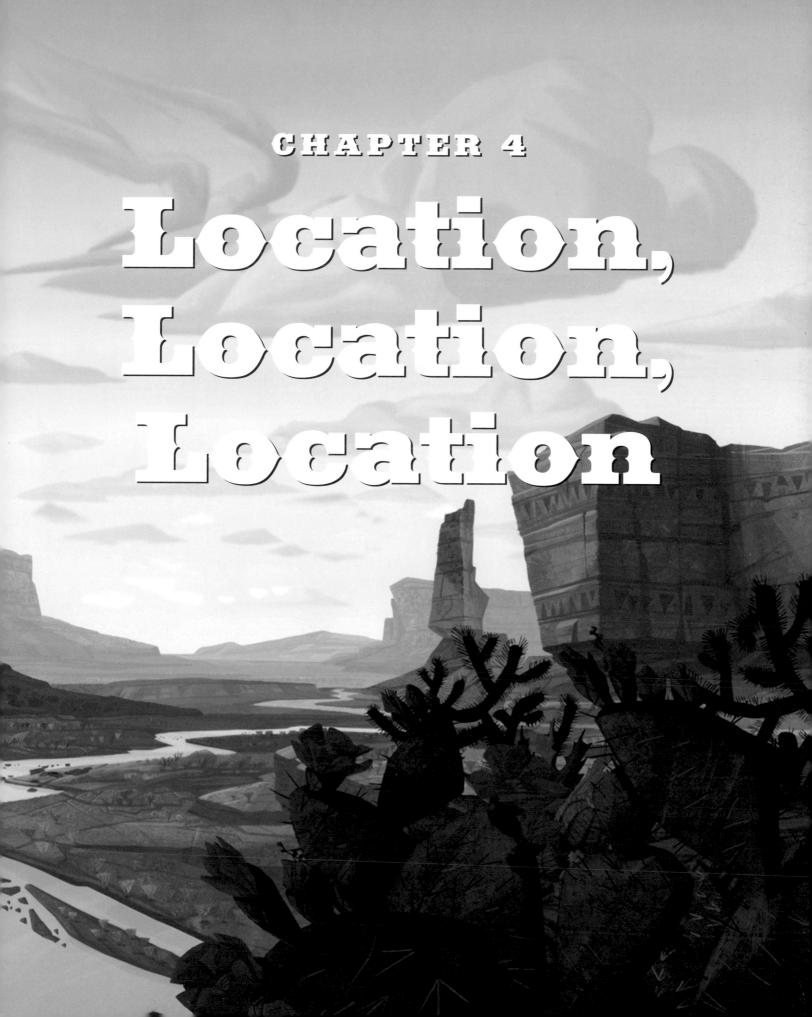

# CHAPTER 4
# Location, Location, Location

## Home on the Range CALL SHEET

LOCATION: THE EXPANSIVE WESTERN WILDERNESS

| DATE/TIME | SEQ. | DESCRIPTION | CAST |
|---|---|---|---|
| Tues./6:00 A.M. | | TRANSPORT TO WILDERNESS LOCATIONS | Maggie, Caloway, Grace, vultures |
| Wed./9:00 A.M. | 4 | VULTURES Maggie, Caloway, and Grace meet up wth a pair of vultures on their way to Chugwater. | Lucky Jack, owls, cowboy chorus, (medic on set) |
| Thur./8:00 A.M. | 0.6 | TITLE SEQUENCE Opening sequence with Lucky Jack. | Buck, Desperados |
| Fri../8:00 A.M. | 5 | BUCK'S DREAM Buck daydreams of greater adventures. | Lucky Jack, coyote, rattlesnake, cowboy chorus, (medic on set) |
| Mon./8:00 A.M. | 0.6 | TITLE SEQUENCE (cont'd) Opening sequence with Lucky Jack. | Maggie, Caloway, Grace, Buck, Rico, cowboys |
| Mon./ 2:00 P.M. | 10 | COWS AND BUCK FACE OFF The cows suggest Buck joins them but he decides to catch Slim himself. | Maggie, Caloway, Grace, Slim (as Y. Odel), auctioneer, townspeople |
| Fri./4:00 P.M. | 7.5 | AUCTIONED RANCH The cows pass Maggie's old home which is being sold. | |

# Day 38 **I admit I am sure glad** to get out of the town formerly known as Chugwater, but heading out into the hot western wilderness for the next several days of shooting isn't exactly going to be a walk around the corral. The art department has to redress almost every outdoor setting for us to enhance the cinematic storytelling. Pretty much up until this point, art director David Cutler has been keeping the camera close to us stars on the farm and in town as a way of showing our level of comfort and familiarity with our surroundings. Once we're out in the open West, though, David plans to pull the camera back to include more horizons, putting me, Grace, and Caloway in a more vulnerable context.

But it's more than just camera angles that help tell the story. It's color, too. I met up with Cristy Maltese and asked her about the plan behind the paintbrush. She told me how, as the film unfolds and we go out into the West, the vistas will become much grander. Everything is bigger, better, and as bold and in your face as possible without going over the top. (I can relate to that.) When our characters are off the farm, we're going to see things a whole lot differently.

Well, Cristy wasn't kidding. Once I saw a sea of orange grass, I knew we certainly weren't in Kansas any more! It was hot and hazy without a cloud in the sky. Grace didn't seem to mind. She lost herself in her soulful singing . . . so much so that she was attracting birds. Not just any birds. Vultures! That cow couldn't carry a tune in a suitcase!

# Day 40

**This afternoon, we met up** with a grizzled desert veteran named Lucky Jack who's been cast as our guide when Caloway, Grace, and I venture out into the open frontier. He's a pretty scruffy-looking hare with a peg leg, and was accompanied by his acting coach, Shawn Keller. We heard that Lucky Jack is quite a character, but Shawn has worked with some eccentric talent before, most notably Preston J. Whitmore and Cookie on *Atlantis: The Lost Empire*.

The funny thing about Lucky Jack is that in *Home on the Range* the filmmakers made him decidely *unlucky*. The opening title sequence has Lucky Jack getting into a series of mishaps that clearly set the tone that this film is going to be one wild ride. Today, he took a great pratfall into an owl's nest where he gets a rude welcome from its inhabitants. Young owls can get a little overzealous, and I think they worked Lucky Jack over pretty good.

The directors quickly realized that they're going to have to spread out the shooting of this sequence over several days, to give Lucky Jack time to recover from each of his "hilarious" mishaps.

**Lucky Jack discovers that "Owl's *Not* Well That Ends Well!" with his new feathery friends.**

# Day 41 **I'm not on the shooting schedule for today**

but I still found myself on the set watching the action.

They're filming Buck's superhero kung fu fighter
sequence. (In his dreams!)

As I was searching for a bit of
shade, I bumped into art director David
Cutler and complimented him on the really neat
surrealness of the scene. He told me how
they not only changed the style from a
graphic to an angular look but made it look
like it's not the real world. They wanted
everything to skew from oranges to yellows. Like,
they made the gun orange, for example.

And the darks aren't superdark. Believe
it or not, there are actually no blacks in
the sequence. I told him the dark browns
made it warmer, and he got a real
happy look before wandering off to
check something. The great thing about David and the
rest of the crew is that they're really good at explaining what they do.
I tell ya, I'm learning so much, I'm going to end up designing one of these
things someday. Show everyone my "vision."

Buck's performance was a vision in its own right. Every time he did some crazy move, the directors would shout, "Wait . . . hold that pose!" or "Add a karate chop . . . now . . . no, now!" or "Think Bruce Lee!" Buck's acting coach, Mike Surrey, once described Buck as a well-trained athlete who never gets to play in the game. He just never has the opportunity. Well, in this film, he gets that opportunity and hits one out of the corral.

The directors, Will and John, finally came through with the real vision for the scene, and the rest of the crew saw it through. As I was leaving for my trailer

(there's just so much of Buck I can take), I overheard Jean-Christophe Poulain telling a crew member how the pleasure of this scene for him was that it had no dialogue. The directors wanted slow motion, very dramatic angles, a pushed perspective, pushed scale,

and a pushed design of location that really shows it as a dream location. In this case, the picture definitely tells the story.

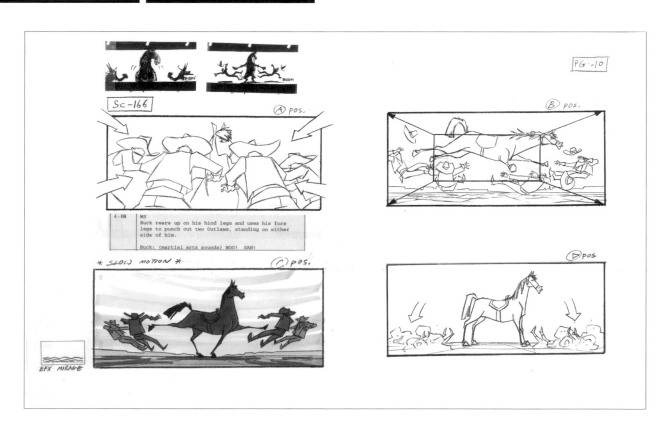

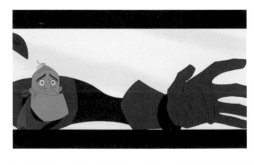  

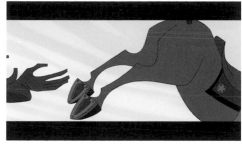
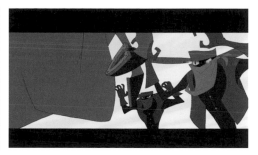

# Day 44 I've got a fews days more of

**downtime** while the filmmakers try to finish off the opening title sequence. Lucky Jack appears to have recovered sufficiently from his scene with the owls so now it's on to run-ins with a wild coyote and a rattlesnake.

Shawn Keller did a great job of preparing Lucky Jack for these scenes. There's a lot of dangerous-looking physical action where timing is critical. And Lucky Jack still has to be able to hit those funny, expressive moments that remind everyone that this is a comedy. I'll say one thing, even with a peg leg that hare can really move.

After they were done for today, I went to my trailer and kicked back with a DVD of *True Grits* and a snack of the same.

# Day 48 I slept in late this morning, knowing that all the scenes we'd do today

would be in the late afternoon at the "magic" hour of lighting. On today's docket was "Auctioned Ranch"—an important dramatic scene for me. I loaned the prop department all my actual ribbons, medals, and awards I'd won over the years. I didn't think it would play so much into my emotions when Grace, Caloway, and I had to walk by my "original" home, but the sheer thought of having all those prizes thrown in some barn, collecting dust where nobody cared. . . .

When I finally made my way to the set, I found visual development artist Karen Keller waiting there for me. She was the one who developed the look to the scene that would

really made it work and had asked to borrow my ribbons and such. She knows, intuitively, how to look at a scene and figure out a way to evoke what the character is feeling. It could be through the camera, the background, or editing. As we walked on, she put her arm around my shoulder and talked about how you can make the locations speak an emotion as much as dialogue or lighting. When I go past my old ranch and remember what things used to be like, there's high contrast. The look is more jagged, more surrealistic. It accentuates the mood. That's a powerful sequence that speaks to the heart of the film.

She's right. It got my stomachs all churned up just thinking about it. But she made me feel a lot better, knowing my contribution would make the scene a little bit richer.

## Home on the Range CALL SHEET

**LOCATION: THE EXPANSIVE WESTERN WILDERNESS**

| DATE/TIME | SEQ. | DESCRIPTION | CAST |
|---|---|---|---|
| Mon./9:00 A.M. | 11.5 | MEET LUCKY JACK<br>Maggie, Caloway, and Grace meet Lucky Jack. | Maggie, Caloway, Grace, Lucky Jack (medic on set) |
| Mon./1:00 P.M. | 13 | JACK ATTACKS<br>Lucky Jack joins the three cows as their guide to Echo Mine. | Maggie, Caloway, Grace, Lucky Jack (medic on set) |
| Wed./9:00 A.M. | | CHOREOGRAPHY REHEARSAL | Maggie, Caloway, Grace, Slim, Willies, cattle herd |
| Fri../8:00 P.M. | 8.5 | BUM STEERS<br>Maggie, Caloway, and Grace meet Barry and Bob. | Maggie, Caloway, Grace, Barry, Bob, Willies, cowboys, cattle herd |

# Day 51

**While Grace, Caloway, and I** continue day after day, grazing, ambling, and chewing cud, waiting to complete the take for our "Meet Lucky Jack" scene, the crew began building the set for Alameda Slim's big number that would be shot in a few days.

For this one, the art department went hog wild! David Cutler told me that the yodel song has the most extreme artwork in the movie. Everything has harder edges, and is more graphic. It's bright and saturated with colors that are constantly changing. The filmmakers wanted to make the song stand out from the rest of the film as a special, unique piece. (Hmmm—should I be calling my agent?)

In this shot of Grace, you can really see the unusual star shapes created for the sky.

Carol Police came up with some really cool design sheets for the stars, such as squares and triangles and wacky shapes.

Then Cristy Maltese informed me that they had opted for theatrical lighting that matches the caricature look of the film. It's not at all realistic. Sometimes they have something lit from the side, and somewhere else, over on the other side, a shadow might be going the opposite way. They did that to vignette the characters within a spotlight area. Okay, I'm definitely calling my agent. When am I going to be vignetted?

# Day 53 Alameda Slim arrived on location today with his dance choreographer,

Dale Baer. Dale's also worked with Yzma on *The Emperor's New Groove* and Doctor Doppler on *Treasure Planet*.

Slim started the day with coffee—black with a squirt of snake venom. Now, there's an actor who's totally inspirational. He loves his occupation. He put on forty pounds for his last movie, *Raging Bullets*, and has been trying to get back to his svelte self ever since. (Of course, the cook's chili isn't helping.) But he's a sight to see: he's constantly rehearsing his dance steps and practicing his yodel.

Now he's shown up early to work on the choreography. Every time I've gone to say howdy to Slim in his trailer, Dale's got him watching some old episode of *The Honeymooners* or a Laurel and Hardy film. Whenever Jackie Gleason or Oliver Hardy dances, Slim and Dale are right there with 'em, not missing a beat.

Later, at a soundstage rehearsal we couldn't keep our eyes on our hooves because Slim's got this way of

shakin' those little legs and feet under that impressive body of his. What a mean dancing machine! He could've auditioned for the remake of *Prance Fever*!

Caloway and I finally found something in common—we're both absolutely mesmerized by Slim's singing voice and find every opportunity we can to peek in while he's practicing. We asked Grace to join us, but she declined because she doesn't think what Slim does sounds like singing—at least not compared to how she sings herself, which she then proceeded to demonstrate.

Ouch!

After hearing her sing when we left the farm, I knew to be prepared for moments like these. Personally, I find that a corncob in each ear works quite well (and serves as a nice place to hide a snack for later).

# Day 55

**The "Bum Steers" sequence.** I'd heard that they were going to use computer-generated images (CG) to enhance the size of the herd, but I was still impressed by the number of cattle they'd assembled when we arrived on the set. At first, Grace didn't realize they were extras for our scene. She thought we'd come across some kind of major bonding ritual. Admittedly, being three lovely dairy cows amidst a whole herd of steer can be a little thrilling. But the real surprise came once we hooked up with Barry and Bob, a couple of good ol' party bulls. Grace thought they were kind of sweet but Caloway, on the other hand, wasn't so sure. While Bob sidled up to Grace, Caloway preferred keeping Barry at foreleg's length. He got the message loud and clear. At first, I was a little suspicious, too. But then I figured, when in the herd. . . . What a bovine dance party that night turned out to be!

After spending time with them, I realized why these two were a lot more animated than the rest of the herd. Thanks to acting classes with Bob Davies and Chris Sauve, and voice and diction lessons with Mark Walton, who storyboarded this sequence, Barry and Bob definitely stood horn and hoof above the rest.

GRACE: **It must be Slim and the Willies!**

(OS) CATTLE: **Slim and the Willies?!**

BARRY: **Don't worry, darlin'—** *I'll* **protect you.**

CALOWAY: **You have exactly two seconds to remove your hoof before I snap it off at the knee.**

BARRY: **Oop! Sorry, ma'am . . .**

BARRY: **. . . I thought you were the blonde.**

**Caloway had two words for these guys: "Cold Shower!"**

| Home on the Range CALL SHEET | | | |
|---|---|---|---|
| LOCATION: **THE EXPANSIVE WESTERN WILDERNESS** (RED ROCK LOCATION) | | | |
| DATE/TIME | SEQ. | DESCRIPTION | |
| Mon./9:00 A.M. | 9 | Song: "RUSTLEMANIA" Slim's big yodel song and dance number. | CAST |
| | | | Maggie, Caloway, Grace, Barry Bob, Slim, the Willies, Junior, the cattle herd |

# Day 60 **Besides slopping it up at the salad trough,** my favorite pastime has

been sidling up to the piano bench where the music scene is happening. Alan and Glenn have done scores of writing, and it's amazing how each song captures the scene whether it's action or drama or laughter or tears. Their collaboration has been truly instrumental to this film.

I was lucky enough to get a front-row seat at the dailies of the big yodel production number, right next to Glenn and Alice and Chris Montan, the president of Walt Disney Music. I was delighted at how well the song worked. The filmmakers had to show that Slim is incredibly good at what he does—that it's quite easy for him to mesmerize these herds without too much effort. There's a good reason that even the best lawmen can't get him. But when you see cows prancing with grins on their faces and making formations in the way you see a halftime marching band, there's something that's just plain silly about it.

And the yodeling was so complicated and so over the top. We all knew that Slim came in prepared to do his own yodeling. But Glenn told me that they found even more yodelers whose agility and expertise would augment him and jack up the song to the level of a virtuoso Pied Piper. Alice pointed out two of the stunt warblers hanging at the back of the room. Randy Erwin's a virtuoso with an incredible ear. The other was Kerry Christenson, who's more of an alpine yodeler. His expertise added a little humor. Alice also told me they even added the eerie sounds of a theremin just for kicks. (That's that cool electronic instrument that you don't even touch to play.)

Getting all those voices to blend was no easy task. Chris told me how he; Frank Wolf, the engineer; and Alan worked in the studio. They'd record Slim singing up to the beginning of the yodel, and sometimes the first yodel note was his. Then they'd add the other yodelers, and occasionally swing back to Slim again. It's quite integrated and incredibly technical.

I know that if I had to yodel anything in this movie, I'd definitely leave the o-a-e-i-oo's up to the y-d-l-d-r's!

# Yodel-Adle-Eedle-Idle-Oo

Music by Alan Menken, Lyrics by Glenn Slater

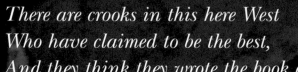

SLIM:    Now listen up!

There are crooks in this here West
Who have claimed to be the best,
And they think they wrote the book on how to rustle.
Well, as good as they may be,
Not a one's as good as me,
An' I barely have to move a single muscle!
They call me mean, boys—
Depraved and nasty too,
And they ain't seen, boys,
The cruelest thing I do:

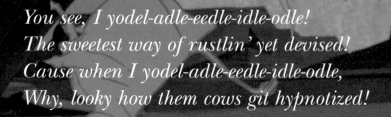

You see, I yodel-adle-eedle-idle-odle!
The sweetest way of rustlin' yet devised!
Cause when I yodel-adle-eedle-idle-odle,
Why, looky how them cows git hypnotized!

WILLIE 1:    He don't prod, he don't yell
WILLIE 2:    Still he drives them dogies well
WILLIE 3:    Which ain't easy when your chaps are labeled XXXXL!

SLIM:    Yes, if yer lookin' from a bovine point of view,
I sure can yodel-adle-eedle-idle
Yodel-adle-eedle-idle
Yodel-adle-eedle-idle-oo!

Here we go, boys! Five thousand cattle in the side pocket!

SLIM:     *Yes, I can yodel-adle-eedle-idle-odle!*

WILLIES:   *A sound them cattle truly take to heart!*

SLIM:     *Yeah, I can yodel-adle-eedle-idle-odle!*
          *An' smack my big ol' rump if that ain't art!*

WILLIE 1:  *He don't rope—*
WILLIE 2:  *Not a chance!*
WILLIE 3:  *He just puts 'em in a trance*
WILLIES:   *He's a pioneer Pied Piper in ten-gallon underpants!*

SLIM:     *Yep, I'm the real rip-roarin' deal to those who moo!*
          *Thanks to my yodel-adle-eedle-idle*
          *Dodle-adle-eedle-idle*
          *I got the cattle out the ol' wazoo!*
                    *Cause I can yodel-adle-eedle-idle-oo!*
                    *Yodel-adle-eedle-idle-oo!*

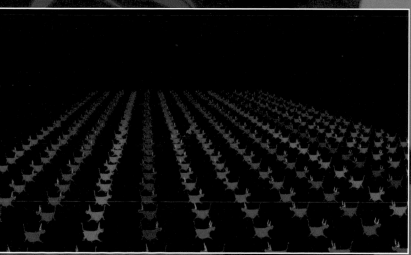

# Day 65

**The scene we were scheduled to work on** originally called for a stagecoach attack, but the idea just wasn't working for the filmmakers. And, it didn't work for a lot of us either—after three weeks under the hot desert sun, we were all running low on vim and vigor. Mustering up the energy for a highspeed stagecoach chase wasn't high on anyone's list of priorities. (And, what is "vim," anyway?) Still, the directors needed something dramatic for this moment in the story. Something spectacular and impressive.

Well, would you believe it? Right about then, it started raining.

I'm not talking about some little fence-lifter or gully-washer. That rain started coming down harder than a goose-drowner. Then the sky suddenly went dark, and a bolt of lightning came out of nowhere and hit a nearby tree. Before we knew it, we'd gotten swept away by a flash flood! Thank heaven for Grace, though. Turns out she was a competitive breaststroke swimmer as a young calf. She saved our hides.

The directors, on the other hand, loved it. They decided a flash flood was just what was needed to heighten the moment. So now, the Effects crew will spend most of the next few days recreating the rain. (Wonder if they have anyone on the crew named Noah?)

When word of what was going on out here got back to Burbank, the then-head of feature animation at the studio, Thomas Schumacher, called a meeting with Will, John, Alan, and Glenn. Tom felt that the film needed a song to play over that moment in which we give up hope of being able to save Patch of Heaven. Alan suggested a rueful reprise of "Little Patch of Heaven." But Tom thought it should be more of a "Where do we go from here?" song. He told them that they should try both ideas but the

most important thing was that he really wanted the audience to feel the complete sense of hopelessness the characters were feeling. Alan and Glenn suggested that there be a *little* hope at the end of the new song. At that point, Tom, Will, and John all put their collective feet down, "No! There can't be ANY hope at the end! Bleak! It must be bleak. The hope will come later when the cows start working as a team."

| DATE/TIME | SEQ. | DESCRIPTION | CAST |
|---|---|---|---|
| Thur/11:00 A.M. | 10.6 | THE STORM Maggie, Caloway, and Grace are caught in a sudden storm. | Maggie, Caloway, Grace, Buck |
| Mon./11:00 A.M. | 10.9 | Song: "WILL THE SUN EVER SHINE AGAIN?" Maggie, Caloway, Grace, and everyone in town and at Patch of Heaven lose hope. | Maggie, Caloway, Grace, Pearl, farm animals, Sheriff, Rusty, cowboys |

# Day 68 **Still shooting the flood scene.** Spirits are getting pretty soggy around here. It's funny how films often reach a point like this. Everybody is tired—and, in this case, wet!

Caloway drew on her experience performing Shakespeare and did her best to inspire the troops with a not-too-shabby reading of the Saint Crispin's Day speech from *Henry V*. I think it would have helped if she'd taken off the little flower hat. It's not exactly what most great leaders of men (or, in this case, cows) would choose to wear into battle. Now I can see why they cast her—later in the story she will deliver the great rallying speech that's the turning point to getting the cows home to save the day. Caloway may have been a reluctant hero in the beginning but her natural take-charge personality has really come through as the film has progressed. I like and admire her more and more—though I'd never tell *her* that!

# Day 72 **I got a call from Glenn Slater today** that's going to get everyone's spirits soaring. He and Alan have written a hopeless song fit for an empty corral, called "Will the Sun Ever Shine Again?" (Makes me tear up, just hearing the title. It's heartbreaking!) And to top it off, Bonnie Raitt is doing the vocals!

I couldn't think of any singer more perfect. The way Glenn described it, Bonnie gives the impression of somebody who's lived all of life to its fullest, and her singing resonates with that sense of hard-earned experience and humanity. You can hear in her voice that she's been in that place of despair, and she's gone through it to the other side and knows there is hope. (So they *did* get in some hope.)

Not only did we finally have ourselves a scene to do, we had a reason to go forward.

# Will the Sun Ever Shine Again?

Music by Alan Menken, Lyrics by Glenn Slater

*Rain is pourin' down like the heavens are hurtin'.*
*Seems like it's been dark since the devil knows when.*
*How do you go on, never knowin' for certain,*
*Will the sun ever shine again?*

*Feels like it's been years since it started to thunder.*
*Clouds are campin' out in the valley and glen.*
*How do you go on, when you can't help but wonder,*
*Will the sun ever shine again?*

What if the rain keeps fallin'?
What if the sky stays gray?
What if the winds keep squallin'
And never go away?

Maybe soon the storm will be tired of blowin'
Maybe soon it all will be over, amen.
How do you go on, if there's no way of knowin'?
Will the sun ever shine?
Wish I could say.
Send me a sign—
One little ray.
Lord, if you're list'nin', how long until then?
Will the sun ever shine again?

## Home on the Range CALL SHEET

LOCATION: ECHO MINE (SLIM'S LAIR)

| DATE/TIME | SEQ. | DESCRIPTION | CAST |
|---|---|---|---|
| Tues./9:00 A.M. | 10.3 | **SLIM'S PLAN** *Slim explains his plan to the Willie Brothers* | Slim, Willies |
| Wed./9:00 A.M. | 15 | **COWS ONLY** *Buck tries in vain to talk his way into Echo Mine while Maggie, Caloway, Grace, and Lucky Jack are let right in.* | Maggie, Caloway, Grace, Buck, Lucky Jack, Slim, Junior, Willies, Rico |
| Thur./9:00 A.M. | 13.5 | **WESLEY ARRIVES** *As the three cows race to Echo Mine, Slim sells the cattle to a city slicker.* | Maggie, Caloway, Grace, Buck, Lucky Jack, Slim, Willies, Wesley, cowboy chorus (montage only) |
| Thur./11:00 A.M. | 16 | **ABDUCTION OF SLIM** *Maggie, Caloway, Grace, and Lucky Jack abduct Slim as Junior and Willies give chase.* | Maggie, Caloway, Grace, Buck, Lucky Jack, Slim, Junior, the Willies, Wesley, Patrick |

# Day 80

**Well, butter my tail and call me a biscuit!** Echo Mine, where Slim will be hiding out with his rustled cows, has been totally transformed. The film's artists turned the place from a dark and dusty hole in a rock (albeit a *big* hole) into some kind of demented amusement park. I asked the layout artist working on Slim's lair, James Finch, to give me a tour, and while we walked, I wondered (aloud) why they hadn't just made it another corral on the surface. Woulda been easier. He

laughed and answered that they came up with the idea to be a reflection of Slim. The tunnels, bridges, and in-and-out spaces show the personality trait of a sick and twisted mind. It's not something that people see on the surface. Very clever.

SLIM: **That's right, boys!**

SLIM: **We're goin'...**

SLIM: **...legit!**

SLIM: **I've been using the revenue...**

SLIM: **...from our little bovine relocation program...**

SLIM: **...to buy up all the adjoinin' farms and ranches.**

The mine interior was so complicated, the crew needed a map just to figure out how to get in and out of the maze! To make things easier, each corridor was painted a different color—green, blue, turquoise, pink. And they glowed—not like jewels, but like something radioactive. Much of that had to do with the theatrical lighting.

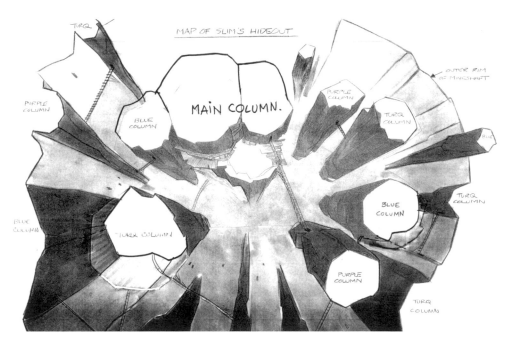

We met up with Cristy Maltese, and I pointed out that there was very strange lighting in the mine. I couldn't figure out where it was coming from. She got all mysterious and said, Yeah, you notice how curious it is? There are times when everything in the mine is dark except for one little spot, and amazingly, that's where all the action is happening. I winked at her and said I'd noticed that and not just in the mine. Watching the dailies, I'd seen how the brights were brighter and the darks darker so we'd pay attention to what the filmmakers wanted us to see. Which was fine with me, because I was definitely reaping the benefit of being in the "spotlight!" Remember, it's all about the cows!

**These color keys by art director David Cutler show all the different colors used inside Echo Mine.**

# Day 81 My first day shooting in Echo Mine! This sequence has Buck trying to

sweet talk his way into the mine past Junior, Slim's rather hefty buffalo sidekick. (If you look at Slim and Junior side by side, they're kind of built the same.)

But Junior wasn't going to take any bull. Well, actually he was—he just wasn't going take any horse!

Then, Caloway, Grace and I show up with Lucky Jack in tow. Since the mine is for "cows only," Buck is shut out while Junior steps aside and lets the rest of us waltz right inside. Of course, it didn't hurt our sneaky plan now that Junior appears to have developed a soft spot for Caloway. That's right—*Caloway!*

I think this scene brought up bad memories for Buck of his early days when he was a nobody and couldn't get into the trendy clubs around town. It was only made worse by his having to watch a scraggly, peg-legged rabbit be let in while he was left standing at the entrance with his reins swinging in the wind.

Once those scenes were done, my bovine buddies and I started getting ready for our big heroic adventure rescue scene and the film's roller-coaster ride of a finale. Wonder if good will triumph over evil in the end?...Wonder if Patch of Heaven will be saved just in the nick of time?...What I *really* wonder is when the lunch trucks will get here!

SEQ 15/71, 81, 82, 83 84, 85 PART 86

I suggested to Buck that the only way he might get into Echo Mine would be to wear Caloway's hat.
He knew enough not to even think about it.

# Day 82

**When the directors,** Will and John, were developing Slim's motivations they came up with several plans for what he was going to do with all those rustled cows:

**Plan A:** Open an Opryland-style theme park complete with hypnotized dancing cows where Slim can perform his yodeling all the livelong day.

**Plan B:** Train hypnotized Holsteins to mine gold nuggets in Echo Mine. The Gold Rush cattle can operate mine cars, smelt gold, and make bullion cubes. At the end of the day have a cash cow add up the profits.

**Plan C:** Become world leader! With his army of hypnotically enhanced cows, Slim marches on the White House and takes over as president of the United States.

The filmmakers ultimately decided on a simpler solution: have Slim, disguised as "legitimate" land baron Y. O'Del, sell off the cows and use that money to buy up all the land in the area. So, all Slim needed was some oily guy to buy the cows. Mark Henn recommended a guy from his acting studio named Wesley. He looked perfect for the part. Turns out he was some hood from Brooklyn.

When Wesley showed up on the set to meet the directors, they told him they wanted a really smarmy guy. They weren't exactly looking for someone with morals. Then Will and John showed Wesley one of the storyboards for the scene.

When Wesley saw how good he looked— or how *bad*—his smile became so bright, we coulda used it during the East Coast blackout. Then I understood why Slim started calling him "Weasely," instead of Wesley.

Then, finally! We were able to get this show on the railroad, capturing Slim to get the reward. And what a show it was! Not to worry, though. Marlon West's visual effects team handled all the dangerous stuff. All the sparks, explosions, and fireballs that are part of "movie magic" never came close to harming a hair on our hides. Well, maybe a little close.

Of course, I performed all my own stunts for the action scenes. Caloway unleashed a hidden strength under her hat and even Lucky Jack got in a few licks.

# Home on the Range CALL SHEET

LOCATION: **ECHO MINE, MACON TRAX RR XING**

| DATE/TIME | SEQ. | DESCRIPTION | CAST |
|---|---|---|---|
| Fri./6:00 A.M. | 17 | **ESCAPE!** Maggie, Caloway, Grace, and Lucky Jack compete with Buck to escape Echo Mine with Slim and take credit for his capture, only to foil each other up and they all end up being caught by the Willies. | Maggie, Caloway, Grace, Lucky Jack, Buck, Slim, Junior, Willies, Wesley, Rico |
| Fri./7:00 P.M. | 18 | **BUCK'S TURN** After discovering that his idol Rico is in cahoots with Slim, Buck turns the tables and helps free Maggie and her cohorts. | Maggie, Caloway, Grace, Lucky Jack, Buck, Slim (as Y. O'del), Junior, Willies, Wesley, Rico, Barry, Bob, Longhorns |
| Sat./11:00 A.M. | 18.5 | **SWITCHING THE TRACKS** Maggie, Caloway, Grace, Buck, and Lucky Jack ride a speeding locomotive towards home and realize they're on a collision course with an oncoming train. | Maggie, Caloway, Grace, Lucky Jack, Buck, train engineer |

ALL: **Hooray!**

ALL: **???**

BOB: **My darlings, nice to see you again.**

CALOWAY: **Oh, no . . . not them again.**

MAGGIE: **Hey! We got a farm to save.**

BARRY: **Take us with you . . .**

BOB: **. . . and maybe we can help each other.**

SFX: *DOINK!*

It was pretty hair-raising at times, but I haven't had this much fun since I rode Thunder Mountain Railroad five times in a row.

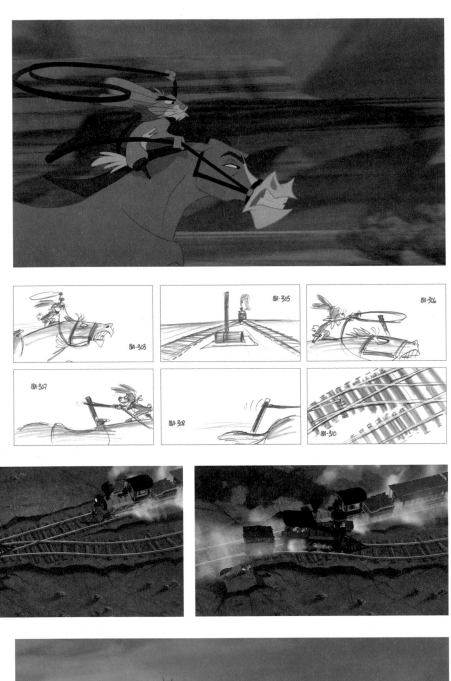

The big finish and the heroes triumph—Cows rule!

# Day 87
**As they say, meanwhile, back at the ranch . . .** Well we did get back to our home—even if we did have to demolish a fence and part of the cornfield to get there! I'd like to say that it was all about the cows, and well, it was—us being the longhorns of the law and all. But I've got to tip my horns to the special effects team, who not only knew how to crash a train in spectacular fashion but also kept the focus on us cows—as you can see in our reflection in Slim's (or should I say Y. O'Del's) eyeglasses.

114

Throughout the film shoot Buck kept jawing about Westerns being all about tough *guys*. But after the way we slam-dunked Alameda Slim, you'd think Buck would finally admit that sometimes it's the womenfolk in Westerns who are the real action heroes. Just look at *Unforgiven*: the whole plot is set in motion by women seeking revenge. Or *The*

*Shootist* with Lauren Bacall. And in *True Grit*, Kim Darby's character drives the story. We are symbols of hope, opportunity, and optimism. Buck may think we're just a bunch of dairy queens, but he wasn't the one holding the milk money at the end of this film. Okay, so maybe it was the Sheriff who literally got to hold the money, but you know what I mean.

# CHAPTER 5
# It's a Wrap

# Wherever the Trail May Lead

Music by Alan Menken, Lyrics by Glenn Slater

*Come with me, and let's go wander*
*Far beyond the wild blue yonder,*
*Out where stars roam free.*
*Though the journey's far from breezy,*
*Stick with me, I'll make it easy—*
*You can depend on me.*

*Yeah, there's a long road before us,*
*And it's a hard road, indeed.*
*But darlin', I swear,*
*I'll get us there,*
*Wherever the trail may lead.*

*Once we cross the far horizon*
*Life is bound to be surprisin'—*
*But we'll take it day by day.*
*Never mind the wind and weather,*
*If we walk that trail together,*
*Somehow we'll find our way.*

*Yeah, there's a long road before us,*
*And it's a hard road, indeed.*
*But darlin', I vow,*
*We'll get through somehow,*
*Wherever the trail may lead.*

*Can't tell you when we'll be there—*
*It may take all our lives.*
*We're headin' for that great unknown.*
*We'll soon be walkin' free there,*
*But 'til that day arrives,*
*At least we won't be travellin' alone . . .*

*And there's a long road before us,*
*And it's a hard road, indeed.*
*But darlin', don't fear,*
*'Cause I'll be right here,*
*To give you the strength you need . . .*
*And through the whole ride,*
*I'll be by your side,*
*Wherever the trail may lead.*

# Afterword

**The end of a picture** is always bittersweet for me. One thing is for sure, though, *Home on the Range* will always have a special place in my heart. It's not every job that includes travel, adventure, and an all-you-can-eat salad trough. Sure, there were plenty of times when it was nothing but hard work—at one point or another, we were all sweating bullets. But when the cow chips were down, it was teamwork that got us through. Never in my prize dairy cow days have I seen a better collaboration among so many exceptionally talented people (and animals). And I've never been happier to share the spotlight with my bovine buddies. I'm going to miss them.

So, what's next? Well, Caloway is headed back to London to star in *The Importance of Being Guernsey-est*. I think this film loosened her up a bit. At the wrap party, she and Junior were dancing up a storm. You could say they were really hoofing it!

Grace wants to open her own talent agency offering holistic solutions for vegetarian actors. It all sounds like granola to me but if anyone can make it work, she can.

Buck just landed the lead in *Equus* at the Burt Reynolds Dinner Theater. In between acting gigs, he plans to teach karate at the Crouching Donkey, Hidden Stallion Martial Arts Center.

During shooting, Slim received an e-mail informing him that he'd been given the green light to direct, produce, and star in a remake of *Beef Encounter*.

I expect Pearl and the Sheriff will remain close. Caloway and Junior weren't the only ones having a good time on the dance floor. Both Grace and I think there's a chance we may see them together again in the future.

And Lucky Jack? He was pretty beat up by the end of the film and decided acting was no longer for him. He asked Jeb if he could move into his barrel for a little while until he figured out his next move. Trust me, that won't last long.

As for me, I'm ready to kick back and relax for several weeks. The Spa de Leche looks like the ticket—I'll be rubbed down, wrapped, and pampered from horn to hoof. By the time they're through with me, I'll be the choicest beefcake on the Grade A list.

Then it's back to the daily grind of parties, interviews, and promotional appearances.

Besides the relationships and memories, the most important thing I'll take away from this experience is knowing that faith, friendship, and fortitude saw us through, and that's something that I'll always have with me, "Wherever the Trail May Lead."

# Art Credits

**Pages 4–5**
Visual development by Michael Humphries

**Page 12**
Story development by Chen-Yi Chang and Cristy Maltese Lynch

**Page 13**
Maggie character development
by Chris Buck

**Page 14**
(Bottom left) Mrs. Caloway rough animation by Duncan Marjoribanks

(Bottom right) Mrs. Caloway character development by Duncan Marjoribanks

**Page 15**
(Top left and right) Grace character development by Mark Henn

**Page 16**
(Top left) Pearl character development by Bruce W. Smith

(Bottom right) Jeb character development by Joe Moshier

**Page 17**
(Top left) Abner Dixon character development by Joe Moshier

(Top right) Rusty character development by Mark Henn

(Bottom right) Sheriff character development by Duncan Marjoribanks

**Page 18**
(Top right) Buck character development by Nik Ranieri

(Bottom left) Buck character development by Michael LaBash

**Page 19**
Buck character development
by Michael Surrey

**Page 21**
(Top right) Alameda Slim character development by Joe Moshier

(Below left) Alameda Slim character development by Dale Baer

**Page 22**
(Top) Willies character development by Carter Goodrich

(Bottom three) Willies character development by David Cutler

**Page 23**
(Top left) Willies character development by Joe Moshier

(Bottom) Willies character development by Russ Edmonds

**Page 26–27**
Visual development by Jill A. Petrilak

**Page 28**
(Top) Maggie rough animation
by Chris Buck

(Middle and bottom) Visual development by Michael Humphries

**Page 29**
(Top left) Visual development
by Michael Humphries

(Bottom right) Visual development by Carol Kieffer Police

**Page 30**
(Bottom) Visual development
by Carol Kieffer Police

**Page 32**
(All) Visual development by David Cutler

**Page 33**
Visual development by Caren Scarpulla

**Page 34**
(Top) Visual development
by Carol Kieffer Police

(Bottom) *Shadows and Sandstone* by Maynard Dixon; Oil on linen; 30 x 20 inches; Courtesy of Medicine Man Gallery, Tucson, AZ

**Page 35**
(Top left) Visual development for *Alice in Wonderland* by Mary Blair

(Top right) Visual development
by Caren Scarpulla

(Middle left) Visual development
by Fred Warter

(Middle right) *Sunburst Cloud* by Ed Mell; Oil on linen; 40 x 40 inches; Courtesy of Medicine Man Gallery, Tucson, AZ

(Bottom left) Visual development for *Sleeping Beauty* by Eyvind Earle

(Bottom right) Visual development
by Michael Humphries

**Pages 36–37**
Visual development by Michael Giaimo

**Pages 38–39**
Visual development by Carol Kieffer Police

**Page 39**
(Bottom) Background by Debbie Du Bois

**Page 40**
(Top) Visual development
by Caren Scarpulla

(Bottom) Visual development
by Carol Kieffer Police

**Page 41**
(Bottom) Visual development
by Cristy Maltese Lynch

**Pages 42–43**
Color key by David Cutler

**Page 44**
(All) Visual development
by Michael Humphries

**Page 45**
(Top) Visual development
by Michael Humphries

(Middle) Visual development
by Carol Kieffer Police

(Bottom) Layout by Karen A. Keller

**Page 48**
Visual development by Carol Kieffer Police

**Page 49**
(Top) Pearl character development
by Bruce W. Smith

(Middle right) Pearl rough animation
by Mark Henn

**Page 52**
(Middle left) Ollie character development by Joe Moshier

(Middle right) Audrey character development by Joe Moshier

**Page 53**
(Top right) Chick character development by Joe Moshier

(Middle) Storyboards by John Sanford

(Bottom right) Jeb rough animation by Sandro Lucio Cleuzo; clean-up animation by Renee Holt

**Page 54**
Storyboards by Mark Kennedy

**Page 56**
(Top) Background by Don Moore

(Bottom) Background by Miguel Gil

**Page 57**
(Top) Background by John Lee

(Bottom) Background by Michael Kurinsky

**Page 58**
(Top) Visual development by Michael Giaimo

**Page 60:**
(Top) Layout by Gary Mouri

(Bottom) Town map by
Jean-Christophe Poulain

**Page 61:**
(Middle left) Townfolk character
development by Joe Moshier

(Bottom left) Story development
by Chen-Yi Chang

**Page 62:**
(Middle right) Townfolk character
development by Joe Moshier

(Bottom) Visual development
by Carol Kieffer Police

**Page 63:**
(Below left) Annie character development
by Joe Moshier

**Page 64:**
(Top) Effects animation by Phillip Vigil

(Middle) Effects animation
by David (Joey) Mildenberger

(Bottom) Rico rough animation
by Russ Edmonds

**Page 65:**
(Top left) Rico character development
by Sandro Lucio Cleuzo

(Top right) Rico character development
by Russ Edmonds

**Page 66:**
(Bottom left) Rusty rough animation
by Mark Henn

**Page 67:**
(Bottom) Visual development
by Carol Kieffer Police

**Pages 68–69:**
Background by Michael Kurinsky

**Page 70:**
(Bottom right) Visual development by
James Aaron Finch and Cristy Maltese Lynch

**Pages 70–71:**
(Top) Visual development
by Cristy Maltese Lynch

**Page 72:**
(Bottom left) Visual development
by Carol Kieffer Police

(Bottom right) Grace rough animation
by Mark Henn

**Page 74:**
(Bottom) Buck rough animation
by Michael Surrey

**Page 75:**
(Top) Storyboards by Christopher J. Ure

(Bottom) Layout workbook page
by Kevin R. Adams and Allen C. Tam

**Page 78:**
(Top) Lucky Jack rough animation
by Shawn Keller

**Page 80:**
(Bottom) Color key by David Cutler

**Page 82:**
(Top and middle) Background by Don Moore

(Bottom) Background
by Cristy Maltese Lynch

**Page 83:**
(Top) Background by Debbie Du Bois

**Page 84:**
(Top) Storyboards by Will Finn

(Bottom) Alameda Slim character
development by Dale Baer

**Page 85:**
(Top) Alameda Slim character development
by Dale Baer

**Page 87:**
(Bottom) Barry and Bob character
development by Sandro Lucio Cleuzo

**Page 88:**
(Bottom) Storyboards by Mark Walton

**Page 89:**
(Bottom) Barry rough animation by
Christopher Sauve. Mrs. Caloway rough
animation by Duncan Marjoribanks

**Page 90:**
(Middle) Alameda Slim rough animation
by Dale Baer

**Page 96:**
Effects animation by Mauro Maressa

**Page 97:**
(Top and bottom) Effects animation
by Dan Lund

(Middle) Effects animation by
Michael Kaschalk, Dan Lund, and
David (Joey) Mildenberger

**Page 98:**
Mrs. Caloway and Maggie rough animation
by Dougg Williams

**Page 99:**
(Top) Effects animation by Allen Blyth and
Peter DeMund

(Middle left) Effects animation
by Michael Kaschalk and Phillip Vigil

(Middle right) Effects animation
by Michael Kaschalk and Dan Lund

(Bottom left) Effects animation
by Peter DeMund and David (Joey)
Mildenberger

(Bottom right) Effects animation
by Peter DeMund and Masa Oshiro

**Page 102:**
(Top) Background by Carl Jones

(Middle) Visual development
by Carol Kieffer Police

(Bottom) Storyboards by Sam J. Levine

**Page 103:**
(Top) Layout plan of Echo Mine
by James Aaron Finch, Kevin Nelson, and
Jean-Christophe Poulain

(Bottom) Color keys by David Cutler

**Page 104:**
(Top) Background by Dean Gordon

(Bottom) Background by Jerry Loveland

**Page 105:**
(Top) Background by Philip Phillipson

(Bottom) Background by Carl Jones

**Page 106:**
(Top left and right) Visual development
by Carol Kieffer Police

(Middle left) Buck character development
by Michael Surrey

(Middle right) Junior character development
by Craig Kellman

(Bottom) Color key by David Cutler

**Page 108:**
(Top) Alameda Slim character development
by Dale Baer

(Middle right) Wesley character
development by Joe Moshier

(Bottom) Wesley rough animation
by Mark Henn

**Page 109:**
(Top) Effects animation by Sean Applegate

(Middle right) Lucky Jack rough animation
by Shawn Keller. Mrs. Caloway rough
animation by Anthony De Rosa

**Page 110:**
(Second from top right) Visual development
by James Aaron Finch

(Middle) Storyboards by Kevin L. Harkey

**Page 111:**
(Top) Storyboards by Chen-Yi Chang

(Middle) Visual development
by Carol Kieffer Police

**Page 112:**
(Middle) Storyboards by Kevin L. Harkey

**Page 114:**
(Bottom four) Effects animation
by Marlon West

**Page 115:**
(Middle left) Storyboard by Kevin L. Harkey

**Page 120:**
(Top) Maggie character development
by Chris Buck

# Film Credits

Written and Directed by
WILL FINN and JOHN SANFORD

Produced by
ALICE DEWEY GOLDSTONE

Original Score Composed by
ALAN MENKEN

Original Songs
Music by ALAN MENKEN
Lyrics by GLENN SLATER

Story by
WILL FINN, JOHN SANFORD,
MICHAEL LaBASH, SAM LEVINE,
MARK KENNEDY, ROBERT LENCE

Associate Producer
DAVID J. STEINBERG

Editor
H. LEE PETERSON

Art Director
DAVID CUTLER

## Artistic Supervisors

Layout
JEAN-CHRISTOPHE POULAIN

Background
CRISTY MALTESE LYNCH

Clean-Up
MARSHALL LEE TOOMEY

Visual Effects
MARLON WEST

Artistic Coordinator
DENNIS M. BLAKEY

Associate Editor
MARK HESTER

Production Manager
TAMARA BOUTCHER

## Story Artists

CHEN-YI CHANG, ED GOMBERT,
KEVIN L. HARKEY, MARK D.
KENNEDY, MICHAEL LaBASH,
ROBERT LENCE, TONY LEONDIS,
SAM LEVINE, CHRISTOPHER J.
URE, MARK WALTON
Additional Dialogue Written by
SHIRLEY PIERCE

## Character Animation

**Maggie**
Supervising Animator
CHRIS BUCK

Voice: ROSEANNE BARR

Animators
TIM ALLEN, JARED BECKSTRAND,
JERRY YU CHING, ANTHONY DE
ROSA, DANNY GALIEOTE, JOSEPH
MATEO, MARC SMITH, MICHAEL
STOCKER, DOUGG WILLIAMS,
MICHAEL WU

**Mrs. Caloway**
Supervising Animator
DUNCAN MARJORIBANKS

Voice: JUDI DENCH

Animators
BOB DAVIES, ROBB PRATT,
MICHAEL SHOW, BARRY TEMPLE,
BILL WALDMAN

**Grace/Wesley/Rusty**
Supervising Animator
MARK HENN

Voices
Grace: JENNIFER TILLY
Wesley: STEVE BUSCEMI
Rusty: G.W. BAILEY

Animators
ADAM DYKSTRA, MARK PUDLEINER

**Buck**
Supervising Animator
MICHAEL SURREY

Voice: CUBA GOODING JR.

Animators
STEVEN PIERRE GORDON, SANG-
JIN KIM, MARK KOETSIER, MARK
ALAN MITCHELL

**Alameda Slim/Junior**
Supervising Animator
DALE BAER

Voices
Alameda Slim: RANDY QUAID
Junior: LANCE LEGAULT

Animators
ANDREAS DEJA, MIKE DISA,
ROBERT ESPANTO DOMINGO,
DOUG FRANKEL, CHRISTOPHER
SAUVE

**Rico/Willies/Horses**
Supervising Animator
RUSS EDMONDS

Voices
Rico: CHARLES DENNIS
The Willies: SAM J. LEVINE

Animators
JAMES BAKER, BRIAN FERGUSON,
JOE HAIDAR, JOSEPH MATEO

**Sheriff/Jeb**
Supervising Animator
SANDRO LUCIO CLEUZO

Voices
Sheriff: RICHARD RIEHLE
Jeb, the Goat: JOE FLAHERTY

Animator
RICHARD HOPPE

**Pearl**
Supervising Animators
BRUCE W. SMITH, MARK HENN

Voice: CAROLE COOK

**Farm Animals**
Lead Animator
JAMES LOPEZ

Voices
Audrey, the Chicken:
ESTELLE HARRIS
Ollie, the Pig: CHARLIE DELL
Piggies: BOBBY BLOCK, KEATON
SAVAGE, ROSS SIMANTERIS
Larry, the Duck: MARSHALL EFRON

Animators
CHRISTOPHER HUBBARD,
CLAY KAYTIS

**Lucky Jack**
Lead Animator
SHAWN KELLER

Voice: CHARLES HAID

**Barry & Bob**
Voice: MARK WALTON

Animators
BOB DAVIES, CHRISTOPHER SAUVE

**Additional Voices:**
Annie: Governor Ann Richards
Patrick: Patrick Warburton
Abner: Dennis Weaver

**Herd Crew**
Lead Animator
MARK PUDLEINER

Digital Herd Technical Director
PETER MEGOW

Key Assistant Animator
LELAND J. HEPLER

Scene Set-Up
SHELDON RAMONES

Rough Inbetweeners: Raul Aguirre
Jr., George Benavides, Casey Coffey,
Wendie Lynn Fischer, Larry R.
Flores, Edmund Gabriel, Mike
Greenholt, Ely Lester, Michael Lester,
Bobby Alcid Rubio, Kevin M. Smith,
Chris Sonnenburg, Wes Sullivan,
Aliki Theofilopoulos

## CAPS Supervisors

Scene Planning: Thomas Baker,
Mark Henley

Animation Check: Barbara Wiles

2d Animation Processing:
Robyn L. Roberts

Color Models: Karen Comella

Paint/Final Check:
Hortensia M. Casagran

Compositing/Digital file services:
James "JR" Russell

Digital Film Print: Brandy Hill,
William Fadness

Post Production Manager:
Bérénice Robinson

Assistant Artistic Coordinator:
Kimberley A. Cope

## Visual Development & Character Design

Character Stylist: Joe Moshier

Character Sculptures:
Raffaello Vecchione

Visual Development Artists: Mike
Gabriel, Michael Giaimo, Michael
Humphries, Karen A. Keller, Jill A.
Petrilak, Carol Kieffer Police, Caren
Scarpulla, Christopher J. Ure, Fred
Warter

## Layout

Layout Stylist: Carol Kieffer Police

Assistant Head of Layout:
Kevin R. Adams

Journeymen: Jeff Beazley, Trish
Coveney-Rees, Dan Hansen, Karen A.
Keller, Emil Mitev, Rick Moore, Gary
Mouri, Kevin Nelson, Jeff Purves,
Tom Shannon, Allen C. Tam

Technical directors: Craig Caton-
Largent, Chris Keene

Key Assistants: Ray Chen, Craig
Elliott, James Aaron Finch, Lam
Hoang, Yong-Hong Zhong

Assistants: Brian Kesinger, Julio
Leon, Craig Sellars, Lisa Souza,
Kevyn Wallace, Will Weston

Lead Software Technical Director:
Eric Powers

Scene Set-Up: Jennifer Behnke

Blue Sketch: Madlyn Zusmer O'Neill,
Monica Albracht Marroquin

## Backgrounds

Jennifer K. Ando, Sunny
Apinchapong, Doug Ball, Debbie Du
Bois, Miguel Gil, Dean Gordon, Carl
Jones, Michael Kurinsky, John Lee,
William Lorencz, Jerry Loveland,
James J. Martin, Kelly McGraw,
Gregory C. Miller, Don Moore, Philip
Phillipson, Daniel Read, Leonard
Robledo, George Taylor, Maryann
Thomas, Thomas Woodington

Digital Touch-Up Artist:
Christine Laubach

## Clean-Up Animation

**Maggie**
Lead Key: Marianne Tucker

Key Assistants: Debra Armstrong,
Susan Lantz, Lieve Miessen, Don
Parmele, Natasha Dukelski Selfridge

Assistants: Scott Anderson, Daniel
Yoontaek Lim, Bernadette Moley,
Steven K. Thompson

Breakdown: Regina Conroy,
Cynthia Landeros

Inbetweener: Suzanne F. Hirota

**Mrs. Caloway**
Lead Key: Nancy E. Kniep

Key Assistants: Margie Daniels, Lee Dunkman, Akemi Gutierrez, Dorothea Baker Paul, Richard D. Rocha

Assistants: Kevin M. Grow, Mary-Jean Repchuk

Breakdown: Christenson M. Casugo, Al Salgado, Wm. John Thinnes

Inbetweeners: Thomas Estrada, James Anthony Marquez

**Grace/Wesley/Rusty**
Lead Key: June M. Fujimoto

Key Assistants: Sean Gallimore, Juliet Stroud-Duncan, Trevor Tamboline

Assistants: Dietz Toshio Ichishita, Mary Measures, Doug Post

Breakdown: Jody Kooistra, Tao Huu Nguyen

Inbetweeners: James Burks, Margaret "Mac" Spada, Kimberly Moriki Zamlich

**Buck/Pearl**
Lead Key: Ginny Parmele

Key Assistants: Inna Chon, Brian B. McKim, Jacqueline Sanchez

Assistants: Kris Heller, Denise Meehan, Annette Morel

Breakdown: Patricia Ann Billings-Malone, Cliff Freitas, Yoon Sook Nam

Inbetweener: Taik Lee

**Slim/Junior**
Lead Key: Ruben Procopio

Key Assistants: Michael G. McKinney, Eric Pigors, Alex Topete

Assistant: Todd H. Ammons

Breakdown: Frank F. Dietz, Gary J. Myers, David E. Recinos

Inbetweener: Drew Adams

**Willies/Horses**
Lead Key: Bill Berg

Associate Lead Key: Kaaren Lundeen

Key Assistant: Merry Kanawyer Clingen

Assistant: Marty Schwartz

Breakdown: Nickolas M. Frangos

**Lucky Jack/Rico**
Lead key: Emily Jiuliano

Key assistants: Steve Lubin, Terry Naughton, Dan Tanaka

Assistants: Brigitte T. Franzka-Fritz, Arturo Alejandro Hernandez

Breakdown: Christopher Gerard Darroca

Inbetweeners: Raymond Flores Fabular, Daniel Schier

**Sheriff/Jeb/Pearl/Vultures**
Lead key: Renee Holt

Key Assistants: Marcia Kimura Dougherty, Myung Kang Teague, Eunice (Eun Ok) Yu, Assistant, Teresa Eidenbock

Breakdown: Allison Renna

Inbetweener: Ryan Carlson

**Farm Animals**
Lead Key: Edward R. Gutierrez

Assistants: Diana Coco, Jan Naylor

**Miscellaneous**
Lead Key: Martin Korth

Key Assistants: Tony Anselmo, Wes Chun, Jesus Cortes, Allison Hollen, Calvin Le Duc, Marsha W.J. Park-Yum, Dana M. Reemes, Stephan Zupkas

Assistants: Chan Woo Jung, Yung Soo Kim, Miriam McDonnell, Susan Y. Sugita

Breakdown: Chang Yei Cho, Steve Lenze

**Digital Herd**

Look Development Technical Directors: Iva S. Itchevska, Heather Pritchett

**Visual Effects Animation**

Visual Effects Animators: Sean Applegate, John Armstrong, Gordon Baker, Allen Blyth, Dan Chaika, Peter DeMund, Michael Cadwallader Jones, Ted C. Kierscey, Cynthia Neill Knizek, Dorse A. Lanpher, Dan Lund, James DeValera Mansfield, Mauro Maressa, David (Joey) Mildenberger, Steve Moore, Mark Myer, Masa Oshiro, Tonya Ramsey, Phillip Vigil

Supervising Animator Digital Effects: Michael Kaschalk

Effects Key Assistants: Marko Barrows, Ty Elliott, Ray Hofstedt, Elizabeth Holmes, David Kcenich, Joseph Christopher Pepe, Peter Francis Pepe Jr., Steve Starr, Amanda J. Talbot, Michael Anthony Toth, John Tucker

Effects Assistants: Kim Burk, Van Shirvanian

Effects Breakdown: Virgilio John Aquino, Steve Filatro, Kristin K. Fong Lukavsky, Jean-Paul Orpinas, Philip Pignotti, Nicole A. Zamora-Redson

Scene Set-Up: Derrick Huckvale, Jason G. Salata

**Editorial**

First Assistant Editor: Craig Paulsen

Avid Assistant: Karl Armstrong

Assistant Editor: James Melton

Additional Assistant Editor: Hermann H. Schmidt

**Casting**

Mary Hidalgo, Matthew Jon Beck

Additional Casting by: Ruth Lambert, C.S.A.

**Production**

Administrative Manager: Liane Abel Dietz

Production Accountants: Julianne Hale, Kathleen Marie-Frainier Fredrickson

**Assistant Production Managers**

Editorial: Dave Okey

Editorial & Production: Lesley Addario Bentivegna

Story: Jenn Brown

Layout: Fred Herrman

Animation: Doerl Welch Greiner

Backgrounds: Suzanne Henderson Holmes

Clean-Up: Tim Pauer

Visual Effects: Michele Mazzano

Digital Production: Tina Pedigo Brooks

Sweatbox/Electronic Workbook: Melissa Schilder Allen

Publicity: Kelley Derr

Dialogue Recording Coordinator: Michael Baum

Assistant Manager digital resources: Alan Botvinick

**Caps Management**

Manager Color Models: Holly E. Bratton

Manager Disk Space & Retakes: Brenda McGirl

Assistant Managers Scene Planning: Katherine A. Irwin, Tim Kwan

Assistant Production Manager Animation Check: Cathy Leahy

Assistant Manager Disk Space and Retakes: Ben Lemon

Assistant Manager Camera: Stephanie C. Herrman

**Scene Planning**

Show Lead: Cynthia Goode

Scene Planners: S. J. Bleick, Glen Claybrook, Annamarie Costa, Ronald J. Jackson, Faye Tipton Johnson, David J. Link, Scott McCartor

Scene Planning & Efx Data Entry: Laura L. Jaime, Monica Dollison

**Animation Check**

Assistant supervisor: Karen S. Paat

Animation Checkers: Janette Hulett, Denise M. Mitchell, Helen O'Flynn, Gary G. Shafer, Mavis Shafer, Karen Somerville

**2d Animation Processing**

Assistant Supervisors: Gareth P. Fishbaugh, Karen N. China

Digital Mark-Up: Lynnette E. Cullen

2d Animation Processors: Jo Ann Breuer, Robert Lizardo, Michael Alan McFerren, Richard J. McFerren

**Color Models**

Assistant Supervisor: Ann Marie Sorensen

Show Lead: Barbara Lynn Hamane

Color Stylists: Penny Coulter, Maria Gonzalez, Debbie Jorgensborg, Heidi Lin Mahoney

Look Development Technical Director: Charles Colladay

**Paint**

Assistant Supervisors: Irma Velez, Russell Blandino, Phyllis Estelle Fields

Color Model Mark-Up: Bill Andres, Beth Ann McCoy-Gee, Grace H. Shirado, David J. Zywicki

Registration: Karan Lee-Storr, Leyla C. Amaro Nodas

Paint Mark-Up: Carmen Regina Alvarez, Roberta Lee Borchardt, Casey Clayton, Patricia L. Gold, Bonnie A. Ramsey, Myrian Ferron Tello

Painters: Carmen Sanderson, Joyce Alexander, Kirk Axtell II, Joey Calderon, Janice M. Caston, Robert Dettloff, Michael Foley, Debbie Green, Vernette Griffee, Debbie Henson, David Karp, Angelika R. Katz, Kukhee Lee, Deborah Jane Mooneyham, Margarito Murillo, Ofra Afuta Naylor, Karen Lynne Nugent, Rosalinde Praamsma, Yolanda Rearick, Ania Rubisz, Christine Schultz, Heidi Woodward Shellhorn, Roxanne M. Taylor, Tami Terusa, Britt-Marie Van Der Nagel

**Final Check**

Assistant Supervisor: Teri N. McDonald

Final Checkers: Lea Dahlen, Misoon Kim, Sally-Anne King, Catherine Mirkovich-Peterson

**Caps Compositing**

Assistant Supervisor Compositing: Timothy B. Gales

Digital File Services: Joseph Pfening, Kent Gordon

**Film and Digital Services**

Technical Supervisor: Christopher W. Gee

Camera/Film Recorder Operators:
John D. Aardal, Bill Aylsworth, David Booth, Marc Canas, John Derderian, Jennie Kepenek Mouzis

Color Timer: Bruce Tauscher

Reuse & Stock librarian:
Vicki L. Casper

**Music**

"(You Ain't) Home On The Range" and "Home On The Range (Echo Mine Reprise)"
Performed by Tim Blevins, Gregory Jbara, William H. Parry, Wilbur Pauley, Peter Samuel

"Little Patch Of Heaven" and "Little Patch Of Heaven (Finale)"
Performed by k. d. lang
k. d. lang appears courtesy of Warner Bros. Records

"Yodle-Adle-Eedle-Idle-Oo"
Slim performed by Randy Quaid
Yodeling by Randy Erwin, Kerry Christenson
Willie Brothers performed by David Burnham, Jason Graae, Gregory Jbara

"Will The Sun Ever Shine Again"
Performed by Bonnie Raitt
Bonnie Raitt appears courtesy of Capitol Records

"Wherever The Trail May Lead"
Performed by Tim McGraw
Produced by Byron Gallimore and Tim McGraw
Strings and woodwinds arranged and conducted by David Campbell
Recorded by Ricky Cobble and Joe Chiccarelli
Mixed by Mike Shipley
Tim McGraw appears courtesy of Curb Records

"Anytime You Need A Friend"
Performed by The Beu Sisters
Produced by Mark Hammond
Recorded by Billy Whittington
The Beu Sisters appear courtesy of S-Curve Records

Songs and score produced by Alan Menken

Songs arranged by Alan Menken and Michael Starobin

Songs and score orchestrated by Michael Starobin

Songs and score conducted by Michael Kosarin

Vocal arranger and contractor:
Michael Kosarin

Songs and score recorded and mixed by Frank Wolf

Music Editor: Earl Ghaffari

Music Production Supervisor:
Tom MacDougall

Music Production Manager:
Andrew Page

Music Production Coordinator:
Deniece Hall

Songs contracted by Reggie Wilson

Score contracted by Sandy De Crescent

Music preparation: Booker White, Walt Disney Music Library

Additional orchestrations by Douglas Besterman, Danny Troob

Assistant Music Editor: Daniel Gaber

Music Production Assistants:
Joel Berke, Jill Iverson

**Production Support**

Assistants to the producer:
Helen Marie Saric, Stacey Groner

Assistant to the Directors:
Maurice Williams

Assistant to the Associate Producer:
Erica Ann Tang

**Production Coordinators**

Caps Production Coordinator:
Kirsten A. Bulmer

Caps Administrative Coordinator:
Rikki Chobanian

Camera Department Coordinator:
Suzy Zeffren-Rauch

Disk Space & Retakes Coordinators:
Renato Lattanzi, Michael Martines

**Production Assistants**

Saja Kristine Sokol, Dana L. Southerland, Dwayne Colbert, Amy Wong, Debbie Yu, Lawrence Jonas, Karen Kageyama, Rudy Cardenas-Rios, Jeffry G. Georgianni, Nathan Massmann, Lisa Brende, Cindy Leggett Ford, Carolyn Yuka Shaushkin, Debbie Vercellino, John Trosko, Brian G. Smith, Jamal M. Davis, Charlene Moncrief

Additional Visual Development:
Vance Gerry, Carter Goodrich, Joe Grant, Dennis A. Greco, Carole Holliday, Craig Kellman, Marcelo Vignali

Additional Story: G. Keith Baxter, Don Hall, Michael Kunkel, Jason Lethcoe, Davy Liu, Donnie Long, John Norton, Brian Pimental, David Moses Pimentel, Chris Williams, Ralph Zondag

Additional Layout: Mitchell Guintu Bernal, Kenneth Brain, Fred Craig, Bill Davis, Mina Ho Ferrante, Daniel Hu, Noel C. Johnson, Michael Bond O'Mara, Gang Peng, Christopher K. Poplin, Doug Walker, Joe Whyte

Additional Animation:Jennifer Cardon, T. Daniel Hofstedt, Jay Jackson, David Moses Pimentel, Andreas Wessel-Therhorn, Theresa Wiseman, Anthony Ho Wong, Phil Young

Additional Digital Production: Dale Drummond, Joe Kwong, Roberto A. Calvo, Joel Fletcher, Hiroki Itokazu, Alexander Mark, Bruce Buckley, Chris Springfield, Patrick Dalton, Mary Therese Corgan

Additional Clean-Up Animation:
Kathleen M. Bailey, Daniel Bowman, Celinda S. Kennedy, Vera Lanpher-Pacheco

Additional Caps: Nicolette Bonnell, Sherrie Cuzzort, Florida D'Ambrosio, Fergus Hernandez, Gayle Kanagy, Randall McFerren, David Nimitz, Devon Oddone, Eric Oliver, Kathleen O'Mara-Svetlik, Dolores Pope, Saskia Raevouri, Stacie K. Reece, S. Ann Sullivan, Christina Elaine Toth, Arthur Zaslawski

Additional Production Support: Lia Abbate, Andrea Alexander, Leah Allers, Kathy Cavaiola-Hill, Patricia L. Chung, Susan M. Coffer, Maria Gomez Lizardo, Daniela Mazzucato, Mary Jo Boyd-Mille, Melissa Miller, Allyson Mitchell, Colleen Murphy

Assistant Production Accountants:
Danielle Boser, Nancy Guo-Gustafsson, Frank William Knittel, Jr., Lisamarie Worley

**Technology**

Manager, Systems Software Development: Graham S. Allan

Manager, Technical Support:
Mark Dawson

Manager, Media Group:
Christopher I. Dee

Manager, Management Applications:
Kevin John Hussey

Manager, Systems: Jeff Rochlin

Manager, Core Animation Software:
John A. Palmieri

Manager, Digital Animation Software: Steve Poehlein

Manager, Traditional Animation Software: Todd Scopio

Manager, Technical Services:
Mark M. Tokunaga

**Technology Support**

Natalie Acosta, Heidi Marie Andersen, Lorenzo Russell Bambino, Mark L. Barnes, Tina Lee Barra, Hank Barrio, Jason L. Bergman, James Colby Bette, Rik Bomberger, Stephen D. Bowline, Edward "Ted" Boyke, Brad Brooks, Letha L. Burchard, Scott L. Burris, William T. Carpenter, Steven C. Carpenter, John W. Cejka, Kent K. Chiu, Loren Chun, Peter Lee Chun, Ray C. Coleman, Tom Corrigan, Dave M. Drulias, Jerry A. Eisenberg, Christian M. Elsensohn Norbert Faerstain, Thomas J. Fico, Ronald A. Fischer, Megan Jana Fish, David Patrick Flynn, Sahara Elizabeth Ford-Wernick, Carlos E. Garcia-Sandoval, Scott Garrett, Adam Garza, Jonathan E. Geibel, Ron Gillen, Sean Goldman, Thomas Greer, Leo Renay Gullano, Michael J. Henderson, David R. Hernandez, Jay D. Hilliard, Scott Himes, John D. Hoffman, James P. Hurrell, Bill James, Darrian M. James, Michael Lee James, Amindra "AJ" Jayasinghe, Marc Jordan, Kevin E. Keech, Kimberly W. Keech, Michael D. Kliewer, Fred Lacayanga, Catherine Lam, Carl "C.J." Le Page,

Joseph M. Lohmar, John A. Longhini, John Edward Lopez, James Macburney, Michael A. McClure, Dara McGarry, Dayna B. Meltzer, Thaddeus P. Miller, Ramon Montoya-Vozmediano, Ken Moore, Thomas Moore, Jr., Jack Muleady, Marlon S. Navarro, Greg Neagle, Jimmie A. Nelson Jr., David Oguri, Mabel Lim Okamura, David E. Ortega, Alan A. Patel, Tamara R. Payton, Ernest J. Petti, James Pirzyk, Elkeer Zaldumbide Pratt, Ron L. Purdy, Deem Rahall, Julie Reelfs, Brian J. Rodriguez, Valerie Sand, James A. Sandweiss, Matthew F. Schnittker, Stephen J. Serra, Jeffrey L. Sickler, Buddy Smallwood, Christine Anne Sparkes, Clay Speicher, Byron Stultz, Zondra Sunseri, Wendy Ming-Yee Tam, Daniel Teece, Michael Tighe, Bond-Jay Ting, Laurie Tracy, John L. Tsangaris, Roy Turner, Tamara Valdes, Carl H. Villarete, Jon Y. Wada, Lewis Wakeland, Tracy Watada, Matt Watson, Doug White, Howard Wilczynski, Derek Elliott Wilson, Fran Raquel Zandonella, Michael Zarembski

**Post Production**

Assistant Post Production Supervisor: Valerie Anne Flueger

Post Production Coordinator:
Robert H. Bagley

Post Production Engineer:
Michael Kenji Tomizawa

Re-recorded at Buena Vista Sound Services

Re-recording Mixers: Terry Porter, Mel Metcalfe, Dean A. Zupancic

Original Dialogue Recordists:
Daniel I. Cubert, Doc Kane

Supervising Sound Editor:
Mark Hester

Sound Designer: Tim Chau

ADR Supervisor: Jim Brookshire

Sound Effects Editor: Niles C. Jensen

Foley Editor: Albert Gasser

Assistant Sound Editor:
Randall Guth

Foley by Warner Bros. Hollywood

Foley Artists: John Roesch, Alyson Moore

Foley Mixer: Mary Jo Lang

Foley Recordist: Scott Morgan

Dubbing Recordists: Judy Nord, Jeannette Cremarosa

Color Timer: Terry Claborn

Negative cutters: Rick Mackay, Mary Beth Smith

Transfer Operator: Robert J. Hansen

Audio Coordinator:
Christopher Pinkston